POCAHONTAS:
THE PROPHECY OF DOOM

CAROLINE CORBY was born and brought up in London. She studied mathematics and statistics at Bristol University, then became a banker and spent thirteen years in the City, ending up as a director in a venture capital company before deciding to leave her job to spend more time with her young family.

Caroline has always enjoyed history and wanted to find a historical novel aimed at children that would capture her daughters' imagination. After searching without success, she decided to write one herself and the Before They Were Famous series was born. It explores the early lives of some of history's most fascinating characters who, in shifting dangerous worlds, struggle to make their mark and become heroes of the future. Of *Pocahontas: The Prophecy of Doom*, Caroline says: "I was intrigued to learn that a young girl saved the first colony in North America and I had to find out more."

Caroline lives in Hampstead, North London, with her husband and three daughters, aged fifteen, thirteen and eleven.

Other titles in the series

Cleopatra: Escape Down the Nile

Boudica: The Secrets of the Druids

William the Conqueror: Nowhere to Hide

Lady Jane Grey: A Queen for Sale

Julius Caesar: The Boy Who Conquered the World

CAROLINE CORBY

POCAHONTAS

THE PROPHECY OF DOOM

WALKER
BOOKS

First published in 2009 by Walker Books Ltd
87 Vauxhall Walk, London SE11 5HJ

2 4 6 8 10 9 7 5 3 1

Text © 2009 Caroline Corby
Cover design © 2009 Walker Books Ltd
Boy on horse image © Image Source/ Getty Images

This book has been typeset in Usherwood and Tempus.

Printed in Great Britain by Clays Ltc, St Ives plc

British Library Cataloguing in Publication Data:
a catalogue record for this book is
available from the British Library

ISBN 978-1-4063-1373-4

www.walker.co.uk

For Etti

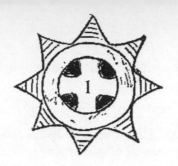

Late Autumn, 1606

"POCAHONTAS! In you go!"

A woman and her granddaughter were standing on the banks of the wide Pamunkey River, an expanse of water snaking slowly through frozen meadows. The easterly wind was bitter and the girl drew her fur cape closer, for underneath she was naked.

"Do I really have to, Keffgore? Can't I have just one day off?"

"No," answered the woman firmly. She was more than fifty winters old and had a weatherbeaten face, shrivelled like a dried pecan, with a gummy smile. Her hair was white and wiry, and she chewed constantly on a lump of soggy tobacco. "All my children swam every morning whatever the weather. Now, come on."

With a sigh, Pocahontas passed her grandmother the bearskin cloak. She was twelve winters old, a short, athletic girl with strong limbs and broad shoulders. Her face was pretty, with wide dark eyes and a snub nose. Like all unmarried girls in her tribe, her black hair was shaved close except for a single plait that dangled halfway down her back.

She dipped one foot into the river. The water was painfully cold but she waded in up to her waist and then dived, startling a shoal of glimmering sea bass.

"Go to the far side and back," ordered Keffgore when she resurfaced. "That'll be enough for today."

Pocahontas had lived with her grandmother in the village of Hatto for as long as she could remember. Her mother died in a hunting accident when she was only three winters old and she had not seen her father, the great Chief Wahunsenaca Powhatan, since she was a baby.

"Come on," called Keffgore. "The cold's getting to my bones."

Pocahontas was soon out of her depth, drifting slightly downstream as she headed towards the centre of the river. Once immersed, she enjoyed the bracing water. Her strokes were strong and quick. In any race she was always the first child to cross the river, and she could dive deeper and stay under for longer than many adults.

To keep warm, she swam harder and faster. Just when her arms were beginning to ache, she felt the slippery pebbles of the far shore under her feet. She clambered up the rocky beach and turned to wave at her grandmother. Then she saw them: a crowd of warriors from her village jogging towards the river, only a hundred yards downstream from Keffgore. The men wore deerskins around their waists. Their hair was shaved close on one side while the other grew wild. Bows and quivers were slung over their shoulders and in their hands they held tomahawks. But it was the colours they were painted that warned her of trouble. Their chests, arms and legs were covered with bright red puccoon root and thick black stripes – the colours of war.

The men splashed into the Pamunkey, carrying large wooden canoes on their shoulders, leapt in, and immediately rowed downriver, towards the choppy sea of Chesepiock Bay. Pocahontas stood shivering in the shallows as the last of the boats disappeared around the bend in the river. She was perplexed. The Powhatan empire was at peace. The wild Massawomecks in the north occasionally raided Chief Powhatan's outlying tribes, but these men were heading south. Where could they be going? *Keffgore*, she suddenly thought. Her grandmother would know; she always knew everything.

Quickly, Pocahontas dived back into the water and as soon as her feet touched the slimy bottom of the shore she called out, "What's happening? Where are the men going?"

"I suppose you'll find out soon enough," said her grandmother, handing back her cloak. "Do you know Japazaw – your father's most senior priest?"

"I've heard of him."

"Well, two nights ago, Okeus came to him in a dream."

Pocahontas was immediately intrigued. Of all the gods,

Okeus was the trickiest. The Sun gave life and Ahone blessed the earth with food, but Okeus often meant trouble. He was a fickle god, difficult to please, easy to offend and never to be trifled with.

"What did he say?" she asked eagerly.

"He warned the priest that a new nation could arise from the tip of the bay and grow so powerful it'll bury us all."

"But the tip is the Chesepiocks' land," Pocahontas said. "Surely Okeus didn't mean them."

News often reached Pocahontas's village of quarrels between Powhatan tribes. The Appocants squabbled with the Kislacks over hunting grounds. The Patawomecks hated the Nansemonds. But the Chesepiocks were different. They dressed soberly and kept to themselves. Pocahontas couldn't think of a tribe less likely to threaten her father.

"Aren't the Chesepiocks our friends?" she asked.

"Some might be, but Okeus has warned there's evil among them," answered Keffgore, spitting out a lump of mushy tobacco. "Your father has decided they must be dealt with."

"How?"

"They'll be killed."

"You can't mean that!" Pocahontas gasped. Only last spring, she and Keffgore had visited Skicoak, the Chesepiocks' largest village, to trade charms and medicines for fresh oysters. Pocahontas remembered an elderly man who'd given her a plum and a couple of girls, only a few winters old, playing with shells on the beach. Would they really all be slaughtered today?

"Keffgore, how could the chief do that?"

"He has no choice. If Okeus warns of trouble, he has to act."

"But what about the children?" asked Pocahontas. "Couldn't they be spared?"

"Children grow up," answered her grandmother shortly. "A chief cannot afford to be lenient. He is acting for all our sakes ... you included."

But the memory of those warriors dressed for battle filled Pocahontas with foreboding. Somehow she was certain that killing the peaceable Chesepiocks was not the right thing to do, whatever Okeus said.

"THEY'RE coming!"

Pocahontas dropped the bloodied shell she'd been using to scrape fat from a hide.

"Let's meet them," she said to the boy working beside her.

Namontack was her oldest friend. In the small village of Hatto they'd grown up together, first crawling in the dust, then daring each other to enter the forest and finally becoming accomplished runners, hunters and trackers. Keffgore always said if she saw Pocahontas, she knew Namontack wouldn't be far away.

He was a stringy boy with a long face, prominent cheekbones and eyes as dark and round as an owl's. His head was shaved and, despite the crisp autumnal air, he wore nothing but a loincloth and a thick layer of greasy hickory nut oil.

"What's wrong?" asked Pocahontas when he didn't immediately jump up.

"I'm worried about Father."

All day the villagers of Hatto had been on tenterhooks, waiting for their warriors to return. Men too old to fight chewed fretfully through their tobacco and short-tempered women shooed their children away.

"Your mother sacrificed a lump of suet, didn't she?" asked Pocahontas.

"Yes, and she cut the fat exactly as Keffgore told her to."

Pocahontas's grandmother was an expert in medicines and spells. She could often be seen hobbling around the forest, a satchel over her shoulder, searching for precious roots and bark. Foxglove was excellent for snakebites. Burning white trillium reduced the risks during childbirth, and if a field wasn't flourishing she'd know just how to mollify Ahone with a gift of tobacco or a string of pearls. At times of crisis she was particularly busy. Most of that day Pocahontas had been banned from their home while her grandmother handed out charms to a string of anxious visitors.

Just then, another woman shouted, "I can see them!"

"Come on," said Namontack. "Let's go to the river, and then at least I'll know."

By the time they reached the banks of the Pamunkey, a crowd had gathered. The approaching warriors looked grim and exhausted. Their morning's paint was smeared and messy, and several had ugly gashes on their arms and legs. Quickly Pocahontas scanned the boats.

"Can you see him?" she asked Namontack.

"Not yet."

The canoes ran aground on the pebble beach and the men tumbled out, wearily recounting their adventures.

The Chesepiocks had been taken by surprise and were massively outnumbered. Despite putting up a brave fight, every adult had been slaughtered and most of the children, and for all this only three Powhatans were killed and eleven injured.

As the last boat emptied, Pocahontas noticed a girl crouching in the hull of the furthest canoe. She was slight, had tattoos on her cheeks and wore her hair in two plaits, in the traditional manner of the Chesepiocks.

Pocahontas turned to the nearest warrior.

"Excuse me, sir, but who's that?"

The man glanced at the cowering girl.

"She was caught right at the end of the raid – about the only one to survive."

Pocahontas gazed at the girl. She must be eleven or twelve winters – just about old enough to be a slave. She turned to Namontack to point her out, but he wasn't there. Quickly, she searched up and down the beach. There he was, at the far end of the cove, but something was wrong. He was unusually pale, his five younger sisters were in tears and his mother had her head in her hands. Pocahontas's heart sank. Something *had* happened to his father.

Frantically, she pushed her way through the crowd. Now she could hear the panic-stricken cries of Namontack's mother.

"Of all the warriors, Kocoum had to be killed. I've got six children. How can I raise them alone?"

Pocahontas knew the family already struggled. Namontack's father had been a poor hunter. By the time he'd paid his tribute to Chief Powhatan of five deer for every one he kept, his neighbours had caught three times as many. It was the same with farming. Somehow Kocoum's fields always yielded too little and he was often forced to go begging for food from the village stores.

"Namontack, I'm so sorry," said Pocahontas as soon as she reached him. "I can't believe it, after all your mother did."

"It's Okeus," he said bitterly. "He never liked my father. And now the family has no hunter."

"The village will feed you," said Pocahontas but Namontack shook his head.

"We can't live off handouts. It's humiliating. I've decided – I'm going to do the Huskanaw. Then at least we can fend for ourselves."

The Huskanaw was the ordeal that every boy had to go through to become a man. Initiates were painted white, the colour of death, and taken off into the woods by priests. Wild rumours circulated about what happened there, for a returning man never spoke of it. It was said they drank a concoction of poisonous roots that drove them close to madness. Many were never seen again, but the successful ones returned after four moons – permitted to farm land, take a wife and, most importantly, join the deer hunt. But these men were at least fifteen winters old, not twelve like Namontack.

"You're not nearly old enough," protested Pocahontas. "Nobody does it at your age. It could kill you."

"I've no choice," he said grimly. "I'm going to talk to the chief as soon as the victory celebrations are over."

Pocahontas was dismayed. *That wretched prophecy*, she thought. Because of Okeus's warning, the Chesepiocks had been slaughtered, Namontack's family was fatherless and he was about to risk his life. Whatever the prophecy had saved them from, could it really be worse than this?

THE morning sky was dull and snow lay on the ground in the shadier patches of the forest clearing. Despite her deerskin mantle and buckskin moccasins, Pocahontas was cold.

"Throw."

She tossed a lump of moss high in the air. It darted this way and that in the biting breeze, but Namontack's arrow of sharpened bone sailed straight through its middle.

"Again."

Pocahontas flung a chunk high to her left, then another to the right, and his arrows easily shot through both.

"Honestly Namontack, you don't need any more practice," she said, rubbing her frozen hands together. "You've hit every one."

"Then throw them higher. I've got to be absolutely perfect to have any chance of convincing Parahunt."

Parahunt was the chief of Hatto. He was a popular, easy-going man whose only failing was that he could never make up his mind. Every morning, after dawn prayers to Ahone, he agonized over where his men should hunt. Each autumn he put off choosing which part of the forest to clear for new planting and at leaf-fall it took him days to decide who should take the village's annual tribute to Chief Powhatan. Typically, he was still wavering over whether to allow Namontack to attempt the Huskanaw.

"A few more then," agreed Pocahontas, for, despite her reservations about Namontack's plans, she could see he had made up his mind.

She began searching the forest floor and soon found just what she wanted – a shrivelled hickory nut. As she bent down to pick it up, a girl walked into the clearing. It was Tassore, the prisoner Pocahontas had seen crouching in the hull of the canoe on the day of the Chesepiock raid. She was now a slave in Parahunt's household.

"Pocahontas, the chief wants you," said Tassore in her distinctive clipped Chesepiock accent.

Tassore's face was sallow and unhappy, a sad contrast to the jaunty jumping fish tattooed on her cheeks. She wore her hair in plaits, refusing to have it shaved like the other girls in the village, and never decorated her clothes with so much as a feather. In every way she could, she announced she was still a proud member of the Chesepiock tribe and would remain one as long as she lived.

"What does he want?" asked Pocahontas. It wasn't often that her half-brother called for her.

Like Pocahontas, Parahunt was one of Chief Wahunsenaca Powhatan's many children. At twenty winters old, their father had inherited six tribes and over the next fifty winters he had gone on to conquer many more. His lands now stretched from the Patawomeck

River in the north to the end of the huge Chesepiock Bay in the south and as far west as the Quirank Mountains. Each time he conquered a tribe, he took from it new wives. During his long reign, he'd married more than fifty women and now had several hundred children scattered across his empire, ranging from middle-aged chiefs like Parahunt to tiny babies.

"The chief would hardly tell me, would he?" Tassore answered.

Pocahontas sighed.

"I'd better go. Namontack, here's your last challenge." And she tossed the tiny nut high into the air.

The village of Hatto was made up of about twenty houses scattered between fields and mulberry groves. As werowance, or chief, of the Pamunkey tribe, Parahunt's home was in the centre of the village. It was larger than the other reed huts and stood between the sacred House of Bones and the central meeting lodge, well-placed for observing all the comings and goings of his tribe.

As usual, Parahunt was sitting outside his yi-hakan, passing the time with the other men. While the women were always busy – spinning twine, farming, tanning hides, cooking, collecting firewood and minding children – the men were often free. At dawn, after prayers, they hunted – trapping beavers and otters, stalking deer or spearing trout and bass in the river shallows – but once the hunt was over they had little to do. Generally they gathered in the village square and gossiped.

"Pocahontas, come with me," Parahunt called out as soon as he saw her.

He had a leathery face, deep-set eyes and stretched earlobes from which dangled two pearls as big as acorns. Like all but the most elderly warriors, he was impervious to the cold. Leggings, aprons and moccasins were for children; for him, puccoon oil, a loincloth and a werowance's loose mantle of shimmering purple and blue feathers were enough.

Pocahontas followed him into the meeting lodge.

"Sit down," he said, pointing to a pile of rush mats near the central fire.

As she settled herself, Pocahontas wondered what all this was about, for her brother was not usually so formal.

"Sister, I have exciting news," said Parahunt once she was comfortable. "Father has sent for you."

Pocahontas was horrified. She'd dreaded this moment for as long as she could remember. Chief Powhatan's children were brought up in their mothers' tribes, but when his sons were old enough for their Huskanaws and his daughters were of marriageable age, he summoned them back to Werowocomoco, the largest town in the empire, where they had only one task: to please him. If they made a good impression, girls were favoured with powerful husbands and boys were made priests, advisers or even a werowance of one of the smaller tribes. If not, they returned home in disgrace. Pocahontas was apprehensive about her stern father and she hardly knew any of her brothers and sisters. Most importantly, her grandmother needed her.

"Parahunt, can't it wait another winter?" she asked desperately. "Keffgore's not young any more. She can't manage alone."

Since leaf-fall, Pocahontas had noticed that her grandmother was slowing down. On chilly mornings her back was stiff and her fingers painful and swollen. Her trips to the forest often exhausted her and she'd begun to doze in the afternoon. For the past few moons it had been Pocahontas who made sure there was food in the pot and wood for the fire.

"Keffgore will move into my household," said Parahunt. "She'll be well cared for."

"But she'll hate it," protested Pocahontas.

She couldn't imagine her grandmother sharing Parahunt's neat yi-hakan with his three wives and their seven children. Keffgore's home was a jumble of jars, pots and baskets full of precious things. She dried rare herbs, roots and plants. She collected alligators' teeth, the tongues of every kind of snake, dried lizards' legs, quails' beaks and raccoons' feet and, although the place looked a mess, Keffgore knew exactly where everything was.

"It will have to happen some time," said Parahunt. "Tomorrow is as good a time as any."

"Tomorrow!" Pocahontas was appalled. "Why so soon?"

"There's a spare bed in the daughters' yi-hakan and Father has chosen you to fill it. And one other thing. You'll be taking Namontack and Tassore with you."

"Why?" asked Pocahontas.

"The gift of a slave will please Father."

"And Namontack?"

"If he wants to attempt the Huskanaw this early, he'll need Chief Powhatan's agreement. It's not something I can decide."

EARLY next morning, when the sky was still grey, Keffgore helped Pocahontas pack her things. She put food for the journey and a sleeping-fur in a bag while Pocahontas rolled up her clothes. She had two sets of leggings, an apron and a spare pair of moccasins all bundled up in a thick bearskin cloak, which she tied with twine.

"I'm ready," she said, not quite believing what was happening.

"You'll need these," said her grandmother, passing over a pouch containing Pocahontas's modest collection of jewellery: pearl earrings, a necklace of pink shells and five rare blue, yellow and red parakeet feathers. "And it's time for you to have this."

From the back of a crammed shelf she heaved down a wicker box. Inside was a fringed dress made from cream deer hide. "You'll need something fine in Werowocomoco. It belonged to your mother. She wore it to her first feast."

Keffgore handed Pocahontas the dress. It was exquisite; the suede was luxuriously soft and was stitched with tiny bones.

"It's beautiful," said Pocahontas. "But I still don't want to go."

"I know," said her grandmother. "But you must."

"What about you and all this?" said Pocahontas, waving an arm around the crowded yi-hakan.

"I've told you not to worry about me. Parahunt is kind."

"But—"

"No, stop," said Keffgore. "You are Chief Powhatan's daughter. You have to go. It is your destiny."

"I could refuse," said Pocahontas half-heartedly.

"And be dragged there instead?" Her grandmother shook her head. "It would be a humiliation. If you run away, you'll be caught. If you turn up here, Parahunt will send you back. You must accept your fate and make the best of it. You're lively and spirited, and the chief likes that. As long as you stay out of trouble, you'll do well. You might even wed a grand werowance."

"I don't want to marry. I want to stay here with you."

"That's impossible," said her grandmother firmly. "The most we can hope for is to meet again."

"What do you mean?" It hadn't occurred to Pocahontas that this could be the last time she would see her grandmother.

"Your father will keep you in Werowocomoco for at least a couple of winters."

"And you must come and visit."

Keffgore shook her head sadly.

"I'm an old woman. My legs could never manage the journey."

There was a tap on the side of the yi-hakan and Namontack poked his head through the doorway.

"It's time to go. The sun's coming up."

"Before you leave, I have one last thing for you," said Keffgore, pulling from her wrist a bracelet of beaten copper traced with ornate, swirling lines.

"I can't take that," said Pocahontas. "It's too precious."

"I want you to have it," said Keffgore, slipping the bangle over her granddaughter's hand. "It will remind you to stay out of trouble. Now go, and may Okeus be good to you."

Pocahontas hugged her grandmother closely. It was too painful to think of never seeing her again. Somehow she would find a way to return.

NAMONTACK, Pocahontas and Tassore jogged one-after-another with bags on their backs, rolled-up furs secured around their waists and leggings to protect them from poison ivy or sharp thorns. Since dawn, they'd been following a well-trodden trail along the banks of the Pamunkey River.

Pocahontas thought nothing of running several miles to the nearest villages of Chickahominy or Youghtanund, but this journey would take two nights and they needed to pace themselves. They ran in silence, each lost in their own thoughts. To begin with, Pocahontas was sad that every step was taking her further from Keffgore and the home they'd shared, but as the landscape slowly changed from dense pine forest to saltwater marshes, she couldn't help feeling a little excited. Tomorrow she would finally meet her father, the great Chief Powhatan, and begin a new life.

As the sun was setting, they reached the landmark Parahunt had described – the point where the Pamunkey River merged with the Mattaponi.

"Let's camp there," said Pocahontas, pointing to a patch of grass. "Namontack, take Tassore to collect firewood. I'll get supper ready."

Perching on a rock, she opened her satchel and pulled out a water gourd and six strips of dried elk, three round flat loaves of corn bread and a block of pemmican – deer meat pounded together with fat and berries. Once she'd spread these out on a flat stone she went to the river bank, dipped the gourd in the water, and took several cool and refreshing gulps. She filled it again for the others, reaching the camp just as Namontack and Tassore returned, carrying a bundle of twigs, several larger branches and a handful of dried leaves.

"Race you," said Pocahontas, and she and Namontack each grabbed a log.

It was a game they'd played many times, battling to see who could conjure the first flame.

"Tassore, do you want to try?" asked Pocahontas.

The slave shook her head disdainfully.

Typical, thought Pocahontas, as she hurriedly eased a twig into a split in the log's bark and rubbed her hands ferociously backwards and forwards, spinning the stick. She glanced across at Namontack. His log was smoking but there was no flame. Good. She had a chance. She spun faster until the palms of her hands felt raw and then suddenly there was an orange flicker, a spark caught and a tiny flame began to burn.

"Done it!" she yelled delightedly just a moment ahead of Namontack.

Soon a fire was blazing brightly and they munched their supper huddled next to it as the sun slipped below the horizon. In no time the sky was black and the night air chilly.

"I suppose we should get some rest," said Pocahontas, unrolling her fur. "We'll need to be on our way by dawn."

She lay down under the warm skin and tried to settle, but despite the comforting crackling of the fire and the gentle lapping of the river she found it impossible to sleep. Her mind flitted between sadness at leaving her grandmother and excitement at what awaited her tomorrow. She tried rolling over onto her side and then heard a muffled sniff. Someone else was awake. Pocahontas raised herself onto her elbows. There it was again … and again. Someone was crying and it was coming from her left.

"Tassore, what is it?" she asked.

"Nothing."

"Tell me. Are you hurt?"

"No."

"Then what's wrong?" persisted Pocahontas.

"I don't want to go to Werowocomoco," the slave suddenly blurted angrily.

"Why not?" Pocahontas knew why *she* didn't want to leave Hatto, but why should the slave care? It wasn't *her* home.

"How would you like to meet the man who killed your mother and father?" answered Tassore, now making no attempt to hide her tears. "And your little brother and twin sister?"

Pocahontas was taken aback. To her, Tassore was just a

slave girl. She hadn't thought of her as a person with her own family and history.

"We were attacked without mercy," continued Tassore. "My father was pulling me to safety when a man split his skull with a tomahawk. I saw his brains spill down his chest. I'll never forget it."

Pocahontas shuddered.

"What happened to the rest of your family?" asked Namontack, who had woken and was listening intently.

"I don't know what happened to Suckahanna, but I found my mother with an arrow in her back, just after my baby brother was shot."

"How did you escape?"

"I ran for the forest but one of them spotted me. I thought he was going to kill me, but he tied me up instead. I'll never understand how Chief Powhatan could be so cruel."

"It was the prophecy," Pocahontas tried to explain. "Okeus warned that a people would arise from Chesepiock Bay and destroy us."

"I know my tribe. We were loyal," said Tassore fiercely.

"There could have been plans you didn't know about—"

"There weren't and you're only defending him because you're his daughter."

"It's not Pocahontas's fault," Namontack protested. "You can't blame her."

"Maybe not," said Tassore. "But whether you believe it

or not, Chief Powhatan made a terrible mistake that night. Somehow Okeus tricked him and one day the Powhatans will pay."

THE sun was low in the sky and Pocahontas was beginning to wonder whether they were ever going to get to Werowocomoco, when a lean craggy man appeared on the path ahead of them. In his hands he held a bow and the arrow was pointing straight at them.

"Stop!" he commanded. "Who are you? Why are you coming this way?"

Pocahontas quickly explained.

"Ah, you're expected," said the man, lowering his weapon. "I'm Rawhunt, miss, your father's senior scout. I'll accompany you from here. It's not far."

They continued along the trail, around a bend in the river and then there ahead of them was Werowocomoco. The town was surrounded by a tall wooden fence and a patchwork of fields planted with squash, maize, beans, sunflowers and tobacco. Its only entrance was less than a hundred yards from a cove in the Mattaponi River where a dozen or more canoes were tied to stakes in the water.

At the entrance, the wooden fence overlapped, creating a narrow walkway that was guarded by four men. They followed Rawhunt through and found themselves in a crowded town with more than a hundred houses, a central square with a huge meeting lodge, a sweathouse and an enormous House of Bones.

"Namontack, you'll stay there," said Rawhunt, pointing to a building close to the town's walls. "It's used by the sentries. They're bound to have a spare bed."

Next he pointed out a slave hut for Tassore. It was one of several, built on a scrubby bit of land. Even from a distance it looked dilapidated and depressing. After all she'd heard the previous night, Pocahontas couldn't help feeling sorry for Tassore. It wasn't her fault that her tribe had been attacked and that she was now a wretched slave.

"Poor girl," she said out loud, as Tassore wandered off looking miserable.

"Don't feel too sorry for her, miss," said Rawhunt. "I'll admit the slave master is tough, but every winter a couple of slaves are adopted by the tribe. She's young. If she's willing, she'll be all right. Now, come this way."

He led Pocahontas away from the grim slave quarters to a neat-looking shelter on the far side of the main square.

"This is where Chief Powhatan's daughters stay. Your father insists on meeting all newcomers as soon as they arrive so get ready as fast as you can. I advise you to look your best."

The daughters' yi-hakan was spacious, comfortable and tidy. Beds lined the walls on either side of a fire. They were a foot high, made from wood with reed mats lashed across them and were just wide enough to lie on. Five were covered with bedding-furs, and had pairs of moccasins and clothes folded underneath them. Pocahontas went to the empty bunk and threw down her rolled-up fur and bag. From her rucksack she pulled the deer-hide fringed dress that Keffgore had given her, grateful that she had something suitable to wear. Next she put on pearl earrings and decorated her hair with the parakeet feathers. She looked neat; surely her father couldn't possibly complain.

"That's good, miss," said Rawhunt when she reappeared. "This way."

He led her to the large reed-and-thatch assembly lodge. It was surrounded by warriors standing ten paces apart and dressed in loincloths, with tomahawks hanging from their waists.

"They're the chief's guard," explained Rawhunt as they approached the building. "Wherever your father goes, they go."

Namontack was waiting by the doorway, his owl eyes wide with nerves. Like Pocahontas he'd changed and was dressed in breeches and his father's bearskin mantle. The cloak was too long and had several shabby bald patches, but it was the finest thing he owned.

"I'll let the chief know you're here," said Rawhunt, rolling up the reed mat that covered the doorway.

Suddenly, Pocahontas felt very nervous. She hadn't seen her father since she was a baby and had no idea what to expect.

At last the scout returned. "You can go in. Good luck."

The meeting lodge was a large rectangular room, lit by flaming torches and a central fire. Against the walls stood rows of men, their heads bald on one side, while the other was covered with long hair knotted with copper crescents, birds' wings and rattlesnake tails that gently clicked and clacked as they moved. All stood in silence, respectfully watching an elderly man at the far end of the room – Pocahontas's father, the leader of the Powhatan empire.

Chief Powhatan was sitting cross-legged on a dais, several feet above the ground. He was wearing an elaborate raccoon-skin robe, the black and white stripy tails plaited into a belt, and a crown of knotted deerskin. His face and chest were painted red and an enormous chain of pearls hung from his neck. He looked older than Pocahontas expected, with deep wrinkles, grey hair and a thinning beard, but his legs were still as thick as tree trunks, his shoulders broad and strong, and he looked ready to pounce on anybody that displeased him.

At his feet a pretty girl nervously fanned him while five young women sat in a semicircle behind his throne. They were dressed in shimmering feather cloaks and copper necklaces, bracelets and rings. Three of them were heavily pregnant. *They must be his wives*, thought Pocahontas. It was strange to think that her mother must have once sat there, waiting for her birth.

The chief raised his hand and beckoned to Pocahontas and Namontack.

"I'm sure he only wants you," Namontack gulped, but Pocahontas remembered what Keffgore had said – that the chief liked "spirited" people. That's what they must be if she was to make a good impression and Namontack was to persuade the chief to allow him to take the Huskanaw.

"Don't be silly," she whispered. "It will be fine. Come on."

Self-consciously they walked towards the ancient chief and knelt, lowering their heads to the ground.

"So this is Amonute. Let me have a look at you," said a loud, gravelly voice.

Pocahontas hadn't been addressed by her birth name for many winters, but she lifted her head slowly and looked straight at her father. His nose was hooked, with huge nostrils and his dark eyes bored into her.

"Are you still called Amonute?" he asked sternly.

Most children earned second names once their characters were established. Namontack was named for his shooting skills, Keffgore meant "Sunny One", while Pocahontas had been named for her playfulness and curiosity. From the moment Pocahontas could walk, Keffgore used to joke that she never knew where her granddaughter was. One night, when she was only five winters old, she disappeared. Keffgore was beside herself, convinced she'd been snatched by wolves or bears in the dense dark forest. A search party was sent out and it was Parahunt who found the little girl far from Hatto. When he asked her how she'd got so lost, she said that she had just wanted to see what was around the next corner. "You're too inquisitive," he'd warned. "From now on you'll be known as 'Pocahontas'. Your name will remind you not to go wandering off." And from that moment she was never called Amonute again. But her father was not to know this, so she answered, "No, sir. I've become Pocahontas."

Her voice sounded ridiculously squeaky; it was the nerves.

"And who named you that?"

Pocahontas took a moment to compose herself.

"Your son, Chief Parahunt, sir."

"Pocahontas." Her father said the name slowly, as if weighing up its implications. "Mischievous, curious and naughty or laughing and merry. That name can be good or bad. Which is it with you?"

"Good, I hope, sir," said Pocahontas, feeling more confident with each answer.

Powhatan grunted, keeping his own counsel, and turned to Namontack. "And who are you?"

Namontack sat up, gulped and then gulped again like a fish out of water, but didn't reply.

"He's Namontack, sir," said Pocahontas, realizing her friend was too terrified to speak.

"Namontack? And why are you here?" asked the chief.

"I'm... I'm..." Namontack stammered, looking as if he might be sick at any moment.

Pocahontas was appalled. At this rate Namontack would get nowhere.

"Parahunt's asked him to make a request of you, sir," she said quickly.

"Can't he speak for himself?"

The chief leaned forward and studied him intently with his deep-set cold eyes. Namontack was now green.

"He can, sir, but he's anxious." Pocahontas ploughed on, not daring to pause in case she lost her nerve. "He wants to do the Huskanaw this summer. He knows it's early, but his father was killed in the raid on the Chesepiock tribe and this is the only way his family won't have to live on charity. Parahunt sent him here to see if you would agree."

There, she'd said it.

Chief Powhatan's eyes narrowed, as though he were mulling over what he'd just heard.

"He's too timid to speak, but he's ready for the Huskanaw?"

There was a titter of laughter from the wives. It made Pocahontas furious. This was so unfair. Namontack might be nervous here, in front of all these people, but in a forest, tracking an animal, there was no one better.

"Sir, I promise you Namontack is an excellent hunter," she said hotly, "and he can shoot better than anyone I know."

Her father looked surprised and Pocahontas held her breath. Had she been too cheeky? Keffgore had warned her not to upset him. But then, to her relief, Chief Powhatan's face began to soften into something like a smile.

"Pocahontas, I like you," he said. "Many of my children are so terrified of me they can barely mumble their own name. You have spirit. Parahunt was wise when he named you. Come and sit near me. Otta, move."

The pretty girl with the fan jumped up. She had long glossy black hair and was ornately dressed in a suede dress sewn with so many shells it rattled as she moved. Quickly she joined four girls seated in a neat arc behind Chief Powhatan's wives. Pocahontas glanced at them; they were all around her age. They must be her half-sisters – the occupants of the empty beds she'd seen earlier that evening.

"Take Otta's place," said the chief impatiently. "Pick up the fan."

Feeling a little awkward, Pocahontas did as she was told and began flapping the thing around.

The chief turned to Namontack. "How old are you?" he asked sceptically.

Namontack was still looking as frightened as a turkey in a trap.

"Twelve winters," he managed to mumble.

"Twelve winters is very young for the Huskanaw and, though you're tall, you've yet to fill out. But Pocahontas says you're a good hunter. Is that true?"

Namontack nodded.

"He never misses," volunteered Pocahontas from her seat at the chief's feet. "He'll hit five birds with five arrows."

"Hmm." The chief looked thoughtful. "Stay in Werowocomoco for a winter. Rawhunt will watch you and then I'll hear what he has to say. In the meantime Parahunt will arrange for your family to be fed from the priest's supplies."

Pocahontas was relieved. Namontack had a chance and her father seemed to approve of her. She couldn't have hoped for a better start in Werowocomoco.

POCAHONTAS and her sisters were woken each morning by Wassacan, a shrewish woman with a hairy mole the size of an acorn on her left cheek and a lone front tooth. It was Wassacan's job to oversee Chief Powhatan's daughters and she took her duties seriously.

Each day began with a swim in the Mattaponi River and then the six sisters filed demurely back into town to weave mats and baskets, sew clothes or decorate pots and dishes, all tasks that Wassacan deemed suitable for girls of their exalted position.

In Hatto, once her chores were done, Keffgore had allowed Pocahontas to do as she wished. She set traps for wild ducks and rabbits, explored the forests, swam in the rivers and dived for pearls. But in Werowocomoco, as Wassacan constantly reminded the daughters, they must never forget who they were and should behave accordingly. There was to be no wandering off, no running, no gossiping – nothing that could reflect poorly on the dignity of the chief.

It wasn't long before Pocahontas missed her grandmother and the freedom of Hatto. To make matters worse, she saw little of Namontack. After completing her chores she spent the evenings waiting on her father, replacing Otta as favourite, and on the few nights she was free she found Namontack was usually away. The scouts combed the woods, estuaries and beaches, and Namontack was always first out and last back, determined to show Rawhunt that he was fit and ready for the Huskanaw.

"You're hardly ever here," Pocahontas complained one evening when she unexpectedly found Namontack basking outside his yi-hakan in the warm spring breeze.

"We need to keep a lookout," he answered happily. "You can't be too careful."

Pocahontas sat down and slapped her forearms, brushing away the mosquitoes which had returned with the milder weather.

"Why? Who do you expect to find?" she asked, more peevishly than she meant. "Father hasn't any enemies left."

Namontack lowered his voice conspiratorially.

"It's not the tribes we're worried about. It's palefaces from across the water."

Just the mention of the palefaces was enough to send a shiver down Pocahontas's spine. Like all children in the empire, she'd grown up hearing the terrible story of how, forty winters ago, at the beginning of Chief Powhatan's long reign, mysterious white-skinned men had arrived in an enormous boat, snatched a child and sailed off, never to be seen again. Ever since, tales of the palefaces were used to scare children. Mothers warned: if you don't do your chores, the palefaces will catch you; or, if you don't finish your supper, the palefaces will get you.

"Do you think they could come again?" she asked.

"I don't know, but your father does. That's why we're often sent to search the Great Sea."

Pocahontas had only seen the Great Sea once. It was the time she'd traded medicines for oysters in Skicoak with her grandmother. The village of Skicoak was right at the mouth of Chesepiock Bay. The bay itself was huge, with many villages dotted along its coastline, but her grandmother said that it was nothing compared to the enormous grey-blue ocean stretching out into the distance. "Where the Great Sea meets the sky," her grandmother had explained, "that is the edge of the world." And yet, somehow, the palefaces had scrambled up over that edge all those winters ago.

"Have you ever seen anything suspicious?" Pocahontas asked.

"No," said Namontack, "but that doesn't mean they won't return. They could be waiting..." and he grabbed her ankle, "to pounce!"

"Oh, stop it," she said, laughing. "You're just trying to scare me."

"Or cheer you up... What's wrong? Is Werowocomoco really so bad? After all, you're the chief's favourite."

"For now," answered Pocahontas. "Father will soon change his mind. Before me it was Otta and before her, Mosco, and once you fall from favour, you pay for it. Just look at the awful marriage he's arranged for Mosco."

At fourteen winters, Mosco was the eldest sister in the daughters' yi-hakan and only yesterday Chief Powhatan had announced that she was to marry a werowance from the far north of the empire. He was over fifty winters old and she would be his third wife.

"Then you'll have to stay favourite," said Namontack, "and when you see someone you want to marry, ask your father to arrange it."

"It doesn't work like that," said Pocahontas morosely. "Anyway, I don't want to get married."

The thought of it filled her with dread. In Hatto, the girls had some choice in who they were betrothed to, but as a daughter of Chief Powhatan, she would have no say.

"Then what *do* you want?" asked Namontack.

"To go back to Hatto," answered Pocahontas truthfully. "To live with Keffgore and be free of my father."

Namontack frowned.

"Pocahontas, that will never happen. You'll have to think of something else."

But the trouble was she couldn't. As long as her grandmother needed her she couldn't imagine being truly happy anywhere else.

POCAHONTAS shaded her eyes as she looked up at the sky. Great flocks of geese, wheeling and honking in the breeze, returned from their northern breeding ground to winter in the marshes and creeks of the huge Chesepiock Bay.

I can't believe I've been away from Hatto for six moons, she thought as she wandered around Werowocomoco.

The light was fading but the town was still busy. Women were building fresh yi-hakans, naked children were playing in the dust and the delicious smell of roasting venison, duck and quail filled the air.

That afternoon Pocahontas had come back from the high plains of the Quirank Mountains. She'd spent spring and summer in Werowocomoco and then, as the leaves turned magnificent shades of red, orange and yellow and the last of the corn was picked and dried, the whole town had decamped to the hills. All over the empire villages emptied for the autumn gathering of food. Some went to pastures famous for their blueberries, huckleberries, wild plums and grapes. Others picked hickories, chestnuts and walnuts in the forests or hunted deer in the northern hills, but all returned to the warmth and safety of their homes before the first snow.

Pocahontas loved the freedom of the autumn migration. There was so much work to be done that even Wassacan had to concede that Chief Powhatan's daughters must help, and so she had spent days roaming through the meadows collecting acorns and berries. But now, with the return of the geese, she was back to the stifling confines of Werowocomoco.

I wonder if Namontack is back yet, she thought, sneaking into the sentries' yi-hakan. He'd spent the season smoking fish in the waters just north of Skicoak and would shortly receive Chief Powhatan's verdict on his readiness for the Huskanaw. Disappointingly, his bunk was empty.

"Where have you been?" asked Otta when Pocahontas returned to their yi-hakan. As usual, Otta looked immaculate. Her shiny hair was decorated with a clump of exotic feathers and two long copper earrings dangled down to her shoulders. "Supper won't be long and Father's asked for you."

Chief Powhatan had spent the autumn travelling from tribe to tribe and that night a feast was being held in honour of his return. Everybody must be looking their best and certainly no one should keep him waiting.

"Don't worry, I'll be ready on time," said Pocahontas as she pulled on her suede dress and put on her pink shell necklace. As soon as she was ready, Wassacan inspected her carefully, her lone tooth sticking out over her bottom lip.

"You'll have to do," she said. "Now, come on. He'll arrive any moment."

The lodge was crowded and uncomfortably warm. Pocahontas and her sisters just had time to settle themselves around their father's seat when Chief Powhatan entered the long-house followed by two tall men, Chanco and Japazaw.

Chanco was a frequent visitor to Werowocomoco. He was the chief's brother and next in line to the throne. He was over sixty winters old and was bad-tempered. Many an evening, Pocahontas had heard him try to persuade her father to attack the troublesome Massawomecks or expand the empire to the south. His aggressive character was reflected in his appearance. His face looked as if it had been chiselled from flint. Unlike his older brother, he wore no jewellery or paint; the only sign of his elevated position was a cape of pristine snow goose feathers that trailed along the ground behind him.

Japazaw, the Powhatans' leading priest, was much more exotic-looking. His head was shaved except for two tufts stiffened with bear's grease and a short mohawk running from his forehead to his nape. A stuffed, dried blackbird – his badge of office – hung above his ear and his face was painted half black, half red, with white circles around his eyes, reminding Pocahontas of a raccoon. Around his bare waist he wore a belt of wolf tails and a live garter snake slithered around his neck.

Once all three men were seated, Chief Powhatan

clapped imperiously and a line of slaves appeared. Each slave carried a plate piled high with venison, corn bread, fish stew or beaver's tail. Tassore was the last in, setting down a steaming bowl of roasted rattlesnake just as the chief began to speak.

"We're here to celebrate our safe return to Werowocomoco," he announced. "Our harvest was good and, with care, we will have enough food to last us until spring. Okeus has blessed—"

Just then there was a commotion at the lodge entrance and Namontack came crashing in. He was breathless and his legs were splattered with mud.

"How dare you attend your werowance in such a manner?" demanded Japazaw, the blackbird swinging wildly.

"I couldn't wait, sir," said Namontack.

"Why? What could possibly be so urgent?"

"Strange boats have landed at Skicoak," Namontack blurted out. "The palefaces are back."

"HOW many are there?" asked Chief Powhatan.

"Hard to say, sir," Namontack replied. He was still breathing heavily after his long run and was trembling at being interrogated by his chief. "More than a hundred."

"A hundred?" rumbled the chief. "Then it's worse than last time."

"And they are all men."

"No women at all?"

"No, sir. And no children."

"What do they look like?"

Namontack thought for a moment. "Like nothing I've ever seen, sir. They have pink skin, thick beards, odd clothes and odder hair – some brown but mostly yellow and one as orange as copper."

"It's just as I remember them," said the chief, and he sat back down looking thoughtful.

A terrible silence filled the meeting lodge. Pocahontas realized that her hands were shaking so much that she couldn't wave the fan. *Stop it*, she told herself. The Powhatan warriors would protect them, but she couldn't help wondering what the terrifying palefaces wanted.

How safe were they, less than half a morning's run from where the intruders had landed?

It was Chanco who spoke first.

"How did they get here, Namontack?"

"In three enormous boats. They're so big they've got yi-hakans built in them."

"And where did you say they were?"

"They've set up camp—"

"Camp?" said Chief Powhatan. "You mean they're planning to stay?"

Namontack could hardly look at the chief as he answered. "It would seem so, sir. They're building a fort very close to where the Chesepiocks used to live – one bay north of Skicoak."

"Are you sure?" asked Chanco, leaning forward intently. "Is that definitely the spot?"

"Yes, sir," said Namontack, wiping sweat from his forehead. "They're right by the mouth of the river."

"Then we must kill them all," said Chanco. "There's no time to lose."

Why? thought Pocahontas, her mind whirring. *Why is Chanco so certain?*

"Don't you agree, Japazaw?" added her uncle. "After all, it was your dream."

And now she understood... The prophecy. Chanco must think that the palefaces were the people that Okeus had warned of – the people who would destroy the empire. And then a shiver ran down her spine. If these foreigners were so dangerous, did that mean the Chesepiocks were never a threat? Could Tassore have been right, that night by the Mattaponi River? Pocahontas glanced at the slave. Unnervingly, Tassore was staring right at her, her dark eyes wide and furious. *No*, thought Pocahontas. *Japazaw and her father would never have made such a terrible mistake.*

But Chief Powhatan must have been thinking the same thing because he turned to his priest and said, "Japazaw, is it possible that in your dream Okeus meant these foreigners rather than the Chesepiocks?"

The priest tugged at the tail of the slithering garter snake.

"No, sir," he said at last. "I'm certain Okeus meant the Chesepiocks."

"I've heard rumours," interrupted Chanco, "that in the south, many moons' travel from here, palefaces destroyed the empire of the Aztecs. We mustn't wait for that to happen to us. We must attack now, while they're weak."

Chief Powhatan sucked his clay pipe and his eyes narrowed.

"Brother, sometimes it is best to leave a hornets' nest."

"Not if it's too close to your home."

"Chanco, that's enough," said Powhatan sternly. "First we must learn the ways of these strangers. Only then can we decide what to do about them. Until then, they must remain unharmed. Does everybody understand?"

"Yes, sir," the men in the lodge answered in unison.

"Good. Rawhunt will be in charge of keeping their camp under surveillance. The scouts will watch them at all times. No detail, no matter how small, will be missed. But, listen to me carefully." The chief ran his dark menacing eyes round the lodge. "I expressly forbid anyone here to approach them. Not until we know that it is safe. Now eat. We must celebrate the harvest or Okeus will never forgive us."

Pocahontas picked up a handful of corn bread, but her appetite had gone. The palefaces were back, and who knew what changes they would bring.

POCAHONTAS was sitting outside her yi-hakan warming her hands by the fire with Mosco and a newly arrived sister called Amonsens.

"Arakum is so awful," said Mosco gloomily. They were discussing the husband Chief Powhatan had chosen for her. "Did you see how stooped he was? And there'll be two older wives to boss me around."

"At least you'll be further away from the palefaces," Pocahontas joked.

She knew it wasn't that funny, but she couldn't think of anything comforting to say. Mosco's husband was repulsive and it didn't help that a piece of catfish stew had dangled from his stubbly chin for most of lunch.

"The palefaces are the least of my worries," said Mosco. "They've been here a couple of moons and they haven't bothered us yet. No, it's Arakum I'm concerned about."

"Perhaps he'll be kinder than you think," suggested Amonsens tentatively.

Amonsens had been in Werowocomoco for only two nights and had the nervous air of a new girl. She was eleven winters old and was tiny, with spindly wrists, knock knees and doe eyes.

"I'm sure he won't," said Mosco. "He has a mean face."

Just then a man walked into the square, heading for the meeting lodge. Mosco flinched. "Oh no, he's back already!"

Chief Powhatan had taken Arakum on a tour of the fields surrounding Werowocomoco and they were expected home shortly.

"It's not him," said Pocahontas. "It's my half-brother, Parahunt. That's strange. I wonder what he's doing here."

"Go and find out," said Mosco, getting to her feet. "I suppose I should pack or I won't be ready for tomorrow."

Pocahontas jogged over, anxious for news of her grandmother.

"How's Keffgore?" she asked as soon as she reached her half-brother.

Parahunt looked mildly pained.

"As well as could be expected... But she does have an awful lot of things and nothing can be thrown away."

Pocahontas could just imagine. It must be awful for her grandmother. If only she could be back in Hatto with her, living in their cosy yi-hakan.

"And how about Namontack and the slave?" added Parahunt, more brightly. "How are they getting on?"

"Namontack's mostly away spying on the palefaces," explained Pocahontas, "and I don't have much to do with Tassore. But you could ask her yourself. She's just over there."

Tassore was kneeling outside the cooking yi-hakan.

Pocahontas waved at her to join them and she disappeared into the kitchen, no doubt to get the slave-master's permission.

"Why have you come?" Pocahontas asked Parahunt as they waited. Her half-brother hadn't visited Werowocomoco once since she'd left Hatto, more than ten moons ago.

"I have good news for the chief and I wanted to bring it myself. Yesterday, I saw two of the foreigners' boats sail away and they've so little food it can't be long before the last one leaves."

This surprised Pocahontas. At this time of year the forest was groaning with nuts, berries and fruit as well as deer, rabbits and turkeys.

"How do you know?" she asked.

"I hid in a tree and watched their camp."

Pocahontas was immediately interested. Ever since that evening two moons ago when Namontack reported the arrival of the palefaces, she was curious to find out more about them. So far, from the long evenings she spent fanning her father, she'd learned that they constantly dug up the forest like squirrels searching for a store of nuts, that they had hairy faces, that they spoke a strange language none of the Powhatans understood and that, so far at least, they seemed inclined to leave the Powhatans alone.

"What are they like?" she asked eagerly.

"Deathly white, short and sickly. They don't look a bit like warriors but they do have miraculous things."

"Like what?"

"Fire-sticks that can shoot branches from the trees, and axes and knives that never break. Look, I took one I found in the forest to show the chief."

From a buckskin bag he pulled out something. It had a wooden handle and a shiny silver-coloured blade. Pocahontas had never seen anything quite like it.

"It's made of stuff like my bracelet," she said, holding up the copper bangle Keffgore had given her.

"But much stronger." Parahunt picked up a twig from the ground. "Cut this and you'll see."

Pocahontas pulled the blade through the stick, easily splitting it in two.

"What is it?" she asked, just as Tassore joined them.

"They call it 'iron'. And look at these." From the same bag Parahunt pulled a handful of shiny beads. They were amazingly colourful – deep reds, emerald greens, cobalt blues and glittering yellows. "Remarkable, aren't they?"

Pocahontas was captivated by the pretty colours.

"You can touch them."

Tentatively, she took a bead. It felt cold and unnaturally smooth.

"Keep one."

"Really?"

"Yes, whichever you like."

Pocahontas's eyes danced over the colours. They were all mesmerizing, but the turquoise bead was brightest of all. It was bluer than the sea and strikingly clear. She turned to

Tassore and held it out for her to see.

"Isn't it wonderful?" she said.

Tassore shrugged her shoulders indifferently. Pocahontas was infuriated. Here she was, trying to be kind to a slave, and this was all the thanks she got. As soon as Parahunt left, she snapped, "Tassore, if you carry on like this, you'll be a slave forever. Who's going to adopt you when you're so miserable all the time?"

Tassore scowled.

"Why would I *want* to be adopted by the people that murdered my family?"

"You shouldn't talk like that," said Pocahontas, instinctively lowering her voice. It was treasonous; her father had people killed for less.

"Is the favourite going to run and tell Daddy?" sneered Tassore. "Pocahontas, you saw that knife. Men with things like that are dangerous. We Chesepiocks never were."

"You don't know that."

"Yes I do, and so do you. I saw it in your eyes the night we heard the news. You're just too much of a coward to admit it." And with that she stalked off.

How dare she speak to me like that? thought Pocahontas. But the awful thing was, Tassore was right – the Chesepiock massacre *did* trouble her. And if the Chesepiocks were innocent, and the prophecy had been about the palefaces, did that mean the foreigners could destroy them? The blue bead glinted in her palm, catching the last of the sun's rays. It was so beautiful. How could a people who'd made something so lovely be evil? *If only I could see the palefaces for myself,* she thought. *Surely then I would understand.*

THAT night Pocahontas slept fitfully. She couldn't forget Tassore's certainty that her tribe had been wronged and several times she woke up from dreams of slaughtering raiders. As the sun rose, she couldn't bear tossing and turning a moment longer so she climbed out of bed, pulled on a loose dress and moccasins, and slipped out of the yi-hakan, leaving her half-sisters snoring soundly.

The sky was grey, the ground frosty and the square eerily deserted. Not a plume of smoke could be seen from any of the yi-hakans. Werowocomoco was still sleeping.

Pocahontas sat down outside her shelter. She wrapped a buckskin shawl around her shoulders but in no time she was shivering and her feet were numb. It was too cold to sit still and so she began to wander aimlessly. She circled the long house, the sweat house and the House of Bones and then, in one of the shabby slave yi-hakans tucked away by the town walls, she noticed an entrance mat move.

A hand shoved out a fur and a bag and then someone began crawling out backwards, as silently as a deer. First moccasins appeared, then breeches and finally two long black plaits. Only one girl in the whole of Werowocomoco had hair like that – Tassore. She must be running away.

Pocahontas crept over and just as Tassore softly replaced the mat she whispered, "Where are you going?"

Tassore jumped. "What's it to you?" she hissed.

"I want to help."

The words came out before Pocahontas had a chance to think. She should be shouting out, sounding the alarm, not offering assistance to a runaway. But suddenly she was certain: Tassore and her tribe had suffered a great injustice at the hands of her father and she must do something to make amends.

"I'd have thought you'd be calling for Daddy by now," said Tassore, her brown almond-shaped eyes flashing. "You're the reason I'm leaving. I thought you were bound to report what I said yesterday."

"I haven't said a thing," said Pocahontas. "But soon the whole of Werowocomoco will be awake. Decide quickly. Do you want me to help or not?"

"Why would I trust you?" asked Tassore sullenly.

Pocahontas gave the only answer she could.

"Because you don't have a choice. Follow me. If this is going to work, we must leave immediately."

POCAHONTAS was surprised by how easy it was to get Tassore out of Werowocomoco. The sentries didn't question her explanation that she couldn't sleep, was going for an earlier swim than usual and wanted a slave to carry her things. She was the chief's favourite and was not to be crossed so in no time they were outside the town walls, heading towards the Mattaponi River.

"Where are you going to go?" Pocahontas asked as soon as she was certain the guards couldn't hear them.

Tassore said nothing.

"I got you out of there," said Pocahontas exasperatedly. "You can trust me."

"All right then," said the slave ungraciously. "My old home – Skicoak on the Chesepiock Bay."

"Why?"

"Why do you think?" Tassore rolled her eyes. "To see if there are any survivors."

"Surely they'd have run away by now."

"Someone might be waiting, hoping another member of the tribe returns."

"But even if that's true, it's too dangerous," said Pocahontas, wondering if Tassore realized how ridiculous her plan sounded. At this rate, she'd be caught and killed by sunset. "Don't you know the palefaces have fire-sticks?" she continued. "Why not go west to the hills where it's too wild to be tracked? Or head south – I've heard there are tribes there who are no friends of my father. They might welcome you."

"Only after I've searched the bay," said Tassore stubbornly.

Pocahontas sighed.

"Do you even know the way to Skicoak?"

Tassore shook her head. "Not from here, but once I've crossed the Mattaponi, I'll find somewhere I recognize."

"But the trail will soon be busy. You'll get spotted and dragged back to Pochins and you know what he'll do."

Pocahontas had seen slaves hobble around for days after they'd been flogged by Pochins, the strict slave master, but that was not the worst of it. At leaf-fall, just after the harvest, a slave had to be sacrificed to Okeus. Surely a runaway would be just who Pochins would pick.

"I know it's risky," said Tassore, "but I must find out if any of my tribe are alive."

Despite the girl's prickliness, Pocahontas felt desperately sorry for her. Tassore was about to set off into the woods all alone in a fruitless search for her slaughtered tribe. It was hopeless... And then, suddenly, Pocahontas had an idea. She knew it was foolish. She knew her father had forbidden it. She knew it was exactly the kind of thing her grandmother warned her against. But she was outside the walls of Werowocomoco without anybody telling her what to do and she had to take advantage of it.

"I'll take you," she said.

The journey there and back could easily be completed in a night and it would help Tassore, but it was more than that... It was something Pocahontas could hardly admit even to herself... That as much as she was terrified by the palefaces, she was also fascinated by them. And here was an unexpected chance to see them for herself, before they left the empire forever, and she couldn't resist it.

"You don't know the route any better than I do," said Tassore.

"Yes I do," blustered Pocahontas, more and more determined to see the strangers. "Namontack has described it to me several times. I'm sure I can find the way."

"And why would you do that?" asked Tassore suspiciously.

"So I can see the palefaces," said Pocahontas. "Now come on before the *real* swimmers arrive."

All morning they followed a trail through the dense autumn forest. Tassore carried the sleeping fur, Pocahontas the bag that contained a small bundle of pemmican, corn bread and a drinking gourd. The grass was long and they had to watch out for nettles and thorns. Tassore, in breeches, found the going easier but Pocahontas's dress offered little protection and her legs were soon covered with scratches.

The path led south-east, away from Werowocomoco and towards a large bay. Three times they came to points where the trail separated and each time Pocahontas racked her brains, trying to remember Namontack's description of his journey. Had he said bear right or left at the turning by the large slab of granite? What about by the fallen cypress? And the pile of stones? Each time she was relieved when she spotted the next landmark.

Around mid-morning they heard the murmur of running water. The path curved round a huge boulder and, all of a sudden, they found themselves at the top of a narrow gorge. Through a thick mist rising from cascading waterfalls they could see a narrow canyon dotted with blueberry bushes.

"I know where we are!" said Tassore triumphantly. "These are the Tussan Falls. Skicoak's not far now."

They entered the gorge, climbing down wet, slippery rocks by the side of the gushing water and then found a trail at the far end of the ravine that descended steeply. It wasn't long before they could smell salt in the air.

"We must be close to where the palefaces are," whispered Tassore. "After the next corner, we'll head into the undergrowth."

They pushed their way through waist-high bracken until they reached a small pond.

"Camouflage yourself," said Tassore, picking up a gloopy handful of mud.

The mud was warm and soft, and smelt deliciously earthy as Pocahontas smeared it thickly over her arms, legs, neck and face.

"Is that enough?" she asked.

"Yes. How about me?"

"You've missed a bit," said Pocahontas, adding a last dab of mud to the end of Tassore's nose. Then they set off once more.

Moments later, Tassore held a finger to her lips, and then inched forwards. They were at the far end of a strip of land jutting out into the bay. On the opposite side, across the rippling water and less than three hundred feet away, was a narrow beach and beyond that the palefaces' camp.

"Namontack told me they call it 'Jamestown'," whispered Pocahontas.

The camp was hidden by a tall wooden fence but on the water, right in front of them, was an enormous boat unlike any Pocahontas had ever seen. Powhatan canoes were built from fallen tree trunks laboriously hollowed out by burning the logs and then scraping the soft charcoal with clamshells. But this boat was bigger than a yi-hakan and was made of planks, with poles and ropes sticking out at odd angles.

"Can we get closer?" asked Pocahontas, desperate to see at least one of the palefaces before she left.

Tassore looked doubtful. "Do you think that's safe?"

"Please."

"All right," agreed Tassore reluctantly. "But after that

I'm going on to Skicoak and you're on your own."

They crawled back through the bracken, off the bluff and into the dense forest.

"Once we've got over that," Tassore whispered, pointing to a lump of sandstone more than twice their height, "we'll be closer to their camp."

They clambered up the rock, searching for cracks in its rough, craggy surface, slipped down the other side into a shady glade – and froze. Less than fifty feet away a huge bear was nuzzling the ground. Pocahontas couldn't believe it; bears usually stayed high up in the hills, fattening themselves all autumn on berries. To make matters worse, this one had shaggy brown fur, a pointed muzzle and gigantic paws... a grizzly bear, the most dangerous bear in the woods. Pocahontas's heart raced. They had to climb back up that rock before it spotted them... But it was too late. The bear caught their scent and suddenly it pulled itself up onto its two back legs, towering over them, and growled, a deep bloodcurdling roar that rumbled around the forest.

Pocahontas and Tassore backed away until they were pressed against the rock, but the grizzly was getting more and more agitated, shaking its huge head from side to side, its black eyes rolling wildly. *If that thing charges, it's going to kill us*, Pocahontas thought frantically. She'd seen what bears could do. In Hatto, a warrior had disturbed a den and had been mauled to death, his body brought back to the village in shreds. She glanced around for something

– anything – to throw. A stone. It wasn't much but it would have to do.

Without taking her eyes from the grizzly she crouched down and grabbed it.

"Tassore, out of the way," she whispered just as the bear careered towards them. Pocahontas threw the stone but it bounced off its shaggy chest unnoticed. Nothing they could do would stop it.

"Run!" she yelled in desperation, scrabbling up the sandstone rock with Tassore right behind her. She glanced over her shoulder. The bear was so close she could see its dripping white teeth. Suddenly she heard a scream – it must be Tassore – and then there was the most almighty bang and something crashed to the ground behind her.

As if by magic, the bear was sprawled out on the forest floor with blood oozing from its chest. Pocahontas was bewildered. What was going on? Suddenly she felt a dread of this place. Something terrifying was happening in this forest. Something beyond her understanding.

"We must get away from here," she said.

"I can't," said Tassore. "You'll have to leave without me. The bear caught me just before it fell."

Tassore pulled her leg forward. Her calf was ripped open from her knee to her ankle. Frantically, Pocahontas tried to remember how Keffgore would treat a wound: clean it with trout lily and then bind it with bark and grass.

"Wait here," she said, trying to sound much calmer

than she felt. "I'm going to find something to help."

But suddenly things got even more frightening – for into the clearing walked a pale-faced man.

13

POCAHONTAS and Tassore huddled together, terrified. The paleface was pointing something at them and shouting incomprehensibly. *It must be a fire-stick,* thought Pocahontas. *That must be what killed the bear.*

The man walked slowly towards them. His eyes were oddly pale, he had an elaborately curled moustache and the strangest clothes – shiny black knee-high moccasins, dark brown britches and a flowing white shirt with a broad starched collar. Around his ample stomach was a tight-fitting garment decorated with an intricate blue and purple pattern, and he had a black mantle and a big, stiff hat with a glossy band of material around the brim. The whole effect was gloomy and frightening.

The man waved a hand at them.

"Tassore, he wants you to get up," said Pocahontas. "Can you do that?"

Tassore staggered to her feet.

The stranger closer now and Pocahontas could see that he was filthy. His neck was grey with dirt, he was covered in flea bites, his fingernails were foul and his clothes were soiled with sweat and grease. Instinctively she recoiled at his smell as he patted her all over with his grimy hands, searching for weapons. *Don't these men wash?* she thought. *What's wrong with them?*

Once the man was satisfied they were harmless, he pushed at them with the point of his fire-stick. His meaning was clear: follow me.

Pocahontas struggled along, supporting Tassore as best she could, but it was exhausting work. In no time her arm was aching but she knew it was worse for Tassore. Her leg must be in agony.

What's he going to do with us? thought Pocahontas desperately. Her father sacrificed his enemies to Okeus. Their brains were bashed out or they were cut to pieces, joint by joint, with clamshells. Would this stinking man do the same?

At last the trees began to thin and they found themselves in a grassy meadow. The foreigners' camp was built close to the water's edge and surrounded by a sturdy triangular fence with lookout turrets at each of its three corners. When they were less than a hundred yards away, the man shouted something and, like magic, a part of the forbidding wall swung open.

They were being taken inside this awful place and Pocahontas had a terrible feeling they wouldn't be coming back out.

14

"POCAHONTAS, how are we going to get away from here?" whispered Tassore as the gate to the Jamestown settlement clanked ominously shut behind them.

The pale-faced man led them into a large yard with several log shelters and four canvas tents. More men were sitting listlessly around, most of them terribly thin and several with hideous swellings on their legs.

Suddenly, a large creature came bounding out from behind one of the shelters. It was waist-high with a short white coat, a long swaying tail, a pointed muzzle and sharp teeth.

"A wolf!" screamed Tassore as the creature jumped up at her, barking noisily. But just then another man ran over, shouted something at the animal and immediately it sat at his feet. Pocahontas had never seen anything like it – a creature obeying a command. What kind of magic did these palefaces have? Could they order the birds from the sky or the fish from the sea?

The new man was shorter than the one who'd captured them, but was just as grimy and had the most extraordinary foxy-coloured beard, hair and bushy eyebrows. *Could this red colour be the source of his powers?* thought Pocahontas.

Was that why the animal sat so submissively at his side? She stole another glance at the creature. Not a wolf, she decided. Wolves were smaller and grey with pointier ears and bright yellow eyes. This was something different, something she'd never seen before.

"Is that thing guarding us?" whispered Tassore.

"I think so," said Pocahontas. She was close to tears. This was all her fault. If she hadn't persuaded Tassore to go so close to Jamestown, they wouldn't be in this mess.

The stout man and the redhead were now talking, their voices rough and guttural.

"I wish they'd get on with whatever they're going to do to us," said Tassore.

"Me too," responded Pocahontas miserably.

At last the two men fell silent and the redhead came over. He was dressed in the same outlandish clothes and had a pair of yellowy hoops in his ears.

"He's going to kill us," said Tassore, but instead he knelt down, pulled her leg towards him and began cleaning the muddy wound with a damp white cloth. When at last he'd finished he smiled and then spoke, and the most astonishing thing was they understood him.

"Me, John Smith. He," pointing at the older man who had captured them, "Edward-Maria Wingfield. Who you?"

Pocahontas was too shocked to respond. How did he know their language?

The man spoke again. "Me, John Smith. You?"

He had bright eyes, turquoise like her precious bead,

and that same unpleasant sickly smell she'd noticed in the forest.

Pocahontas turned slowly to Tassore. "Should I answer him?" But Tassore was too frightened to speak. It was up to her.

"Pocahontas," she replied cautiously, never taking her eyes off the stranger.

He had a feather in one hand and some thin white squares in the other.

"Po-cah-hon-tas?"

The man pronounced her name slowly and deliberately, and then began making marks on the squares.

"Me English. You Powhatan?"

"Yes," she said. "From Werowocomoco."

"Wero-woco-tomo?" he asked.

"No, Werowocomoco," she corrected him.

Once he was sure he'd pronounced it correctly he made more marks with the feather and then he picked up a clay cup of water and dipped his hand in.

"Name?" he asked, holding up a dripping finger.

Pocahontas realized what he was doing: learning more of their language.

"Water," she said warily.

Smith pointed to the cup and then at the ground and the shelters, and each time she told him the words until he pointed at the stiff black thing on his head. Pocahontas shook her head. She didn't have a word for that.

He took it off and passed it to her. It was surprisingly

soft, particularly the shiny band around the brim, but she still had no idea what to call it.

"No name," she said.

"We call 'hat'," he said. "Say 'hat'."

And then he pointed at his white robe, long black moccasins and the creature sitting beside him with the dripping tongue and said "shirt", "boots" and "dog".

"He's friendlier than the other," Tassore managed to whisper, "and he can talk our language. He might save us."

It was exactly what Pocahontas was thinking. They must do everything they could to co-operate.

At Wingfield's prompting, Smith unclipped the shiny yellow hoop dangling from his left ear. It was perfectly circular, engraved with an intricate pattern of triangles.

"Where find?" he asked, holding it up for them to inspect.

"What does he mean?" Pocahontas asked Tassore, staring at the earring.

"I don't know."

They turned to Smith with blank faces.

"This 'gold'," he said, pushing it closer. "Gold, where find?"

And then he pointed at the bracelet Pocahontas had been given by her grandmother and ran his fingers along the distinctive swirling lines, saying, "More yellow than this... Name gold."

Pocahontas had never seen a metal yellower than

copper until now so she said, "There's no gold here."

He translated for Wingfield and instantly the man's flabby face turned red, his pale green eyes protruded horribly and he began shouting. The only word they could understand was "gold", "gold" "gold".

"They badly want that stuff," whispered Tassore under her breath.

"I know. If only we had some to give them."

"Gold? Where?" asked Smith once more.

"I don't know," said Pocahontas, speaking slowly so that the stranger might understand. "I've never seen it before."

Surprisingly, Smith looked pleased.

"I think he was expecting that," she whispered to Tassore. "But the other wasn't. Look at him."

Wingfield was pacing around, gesticulating wildly and raising his fist at Smith in frustration.

Somehow this "gold" has to be our way out, thought Pocahontas and then she had an idea.

"I live in the tribe of Chief Wahunsenaca Powhatan," she said as grandly as she could. "Tell Wingfield, if the chief has such a thing I will ask him to send it to you."

Smith translated and instantly the plumper paleface had a greedy look about him.

"Wingfield say, bring big chief here."

"He won't come," said Pocahontas. "He's far too important, but set us free and I'll tell him what you want."

There was another long discussion between the

palefaces and somehow, despite not understanding a word, Pocahontas was certain Smith was arguing that Wingfield should let them go. Silently she prayed to Okeus, *Please free us*. And her prayers were heard, for at last Smith held out the earring and said, "Take, so big chief know what mean."

Pocahontas couldn't believe it. Quickly, she tucked the earring into a pouch in her dress, grabbed Tassore's arm and together they passed through the gate to freedom.

AS soon as they were away from the fort and into the woods, Pocahontas was overwhelmed with relief. Those palefaces scared her, with their sallow looks, bizarre creatures and strange buildings, boats and weapons. Everything about them was alien, from the "hats" on their heads to the "boots" on their feet. She wanted nothing more to do with them. She had a sudden urge to jump into the nearest stream and wash away their grime, but her most important task was to help Tassore.

"You have to come back to Werowocomoco. You won't survive in the forest with your injured leg."

"I know," said Tassore sadly.

Pocahontas bound the wound as best she could with leaves and twine, found a stick for Tassore to lean on, and they set off. Despite the crutch however, they made painfully slow progress. By mid-afternoon they were only halfway up the steep climb to the Tussan Falls.

"Could you go a little faster?" Pocahontas gently enquired.

Tassore shook her head. She was perspiring so heavily there were rivulets of sweat running down her muddy forehead and she looked exhausted.

"I can't go on much longer. Leave me here. There's nothing you can do."

"No," said Pocahontas simply. Tassore might have started the day as a mere slave but after all they'd been through she was now much more than that. "Let me help you." And, taking most of Tassore's weight on her shoulder, she dragged her on.

As dusk came creeping through the forest, they heard the sound of rushing water. They'd reached the Tussan Falls.

"We'll camp here for the night," said Pocahontas. "It's too dangerous to go on in the dark."

She leant Tassore against a sandstone boulder in a shrinking patch of sunlight. "I'll get you water. Wait here."

Tassore slumped down, her two plaits dishevelled, the colour drained from her cheeks. *I've got to get her home soon,* thought Pocahontas desperately. *It's that not far.*

She dipped Tassore's water gourd into a pool at the bottom of the falls. The water was fast-moving and should be good to drink. The gourd leaked in several places so she hurried back and washed the mud from Tassore's face and arms, and got her to drink a little. Then Pocahontas cleaned herself up as best she could and went into the forest to look for wood.

When she had a good bundle of twigs and sticks, she tied the branches together and then wove bracken into the frame. The shelter wasn't very sturdy but it would keep out light rain and would be warmer and safer than sleeping in the open, where cougars and wolves roamed at night.

Once they'd shuffled inside, they chewed a lump of pemmican in silence and then snuggled under the fur but Pocahontas found it impossible to sleep. Her mind was whirring. How would she get Tassore home, and if she did, how would she explain where they'd been?

At last she drifted off but the ground was damp and chilly. Throughout the night she kept waking up, cold and uncomfortable. Tassore was sleeping just as restlessly. Every time she moved, she groaned and her forehead felt alarmingly warm.

Finally, the sky turned grey. Pocahontas sat up, her joints feeling stiff.

"Tassore, come on."

There was no response.

Pocahontas gently shook her shoulder. Tassore opened her eyes but they were strangely unfocussed and she began to mutter, "Why are they coming...? Where's Suckahanna?"

Oh no, she's delirious, thought Pocahontas. *What am I going to do now?* She couldn't possibly carry Tassore all the way back to Werowocomoco, but she couldn't leave her either. She looked desperately around the shelter and spotted the water gourd. Could cool water help?

She leant over, grabbed it and crawled out into the morning light. But suddenly an arrow came screeching through the air and landed with a *thwang* right in front of her.

"Stop or I'll shoot again."

Pocahontas was trapped.

SOMEONE had found them, but who? The Massawomecks? But it was too far south for one of their raids. Could the palefaces have changed their minds and tracked them down? But they didn't use arrows... It had to be one of her father's scouts, so what was she going to say?

Just then a sturdy boy dressed only in a loincloth stepped out of the early morning mist, his bow pulled taut with another arrow.

"Namontack!" exclaimed Pocahontas, relief flooding through her. "What are you doing here?"

When she'd left, he'd been away patrolling the empire's southern border. She couldn't believe her luck.

Namontack looked as surprised as she was.

"I've finished my patrol and I'm on my way to spy on Jamestown. But what are *you* doing here?"

Pocahontas told him everything that had happened. "And the worst thing," she finished, "is that Tassore's sick. Her leg looks awful and she's got a fever. I'm not strong enough to carry her home. Will you help?"

"I should get to Jamestown as soon as possible."

Pocahontas guessed the real reason Namontack was

reluctant: he needed a good report from Rawhunt if he were to have any chance of persuading Chief Powhatan about the Huskanaw and going against his orders wouldn't help.

"This is an emergency," she pleaded. "I wouldn't ask you if it wasn't. Surely Jamestown can wait one more night."

Hesitantly, Namontack agreed.

Pocahontas crept back into the shelter and gently pulled Tassore out. She was very weak, but by joining hands Namontack and Pocahontas managed to create a makeshift seat. They struggled along as fast as they could. Soon Pocahontas's arms ached but they couldn't afford to rest.

At last they saw Werowocomoco ahead of them. It was still early in the morning and the place looked quiet and peaceful.

"Wait," said Pocahontas, gently lowering Tassore to the ground. "I've been missing since yesterday morning. I can't just turn up without an explanation."

"Tell the truth," said Namontack.

"Father expressly forbade anyone from going near the palefaces."

"You're his favourite. He'll forgive you."

"It's not me I'm worried about. Can't you see what this would mean for Tassore? She's a slave. Why would he forgive her? Her punishment will be awful ... unless you help."

"How?" asked Namontack suspiciously.

"One of my half-sisters – Mosco – left yesterday with her new husband. I could say that after my swim I decided to pick some blueberries for her journey and made Tassore come with me. I know it's forbidden to wander off, but how much trouble can I get into for that? And Parahunt will have told Father it's the kind of thing I do."

"But what about Tassore's leg?"

"Tassore and I are both new to Werowocomoco. I'll say we got lost in the forest, it's easily done. And then we stumbled on a grizzly, she was mauled and, luckily, you found us."

Namontack looked sceptical.

"Please," said Pocahontas. "I can't say we were near Jamestown. Father will get suspicious because everyone knows Tassore comes from around there."

"But nobody survives a grizzly. They'll know you're lying."

"Not if you found us just as we were being attacked," said Pocahontas triumphantly. "You're the best shot in Werowocomoco. We'll say you fired a couple of arrows and scared it off. Tassore was so badly hurt we had to stay the night and then you helped us home this morning."

"Pocahontas, no," said Namontack firmly. "I don't want to lie."

Just then Tassore started mumbling incoherently.

"We don't have time to think of anything else," said Pocahontas desperately. "Her fever's getting worse."

"I'm not claiming glory I don't deserve," said Namontack stubbornly. "I want to take the Huskanaw because Rawhunt thinks I've earned it, not through some story."

So that's what Namontack's worrying about, thought Pocahontas.

"I'll explain and it will never be mentioned again," she reassured him.

"No."

"Please," she begged. "I can't think of anything else. Can you?"

Namontack stared at her furiously. "All right," he said at last. "But don't ever ask me to lie for you again."

And together they picked up Tassore and headed into town.

NAMONTACK and Pocahontas staggered towards Werowocomoco, half carrying and half dragging the delirious Tassore.

"Let's take her straight to Japazaw," said Pocahontas. The priest was the most skilled medicine man in the town. If anyone could save her, he could.

As they approached the narrow entrance in the town walls, Rawhunt came hurrying out to meet them.

"What happened to you, miss? I've got men scouring the riverbanks. And Namontack, why are you here?"

Pocahontas told him the tale she'd concocted only moments before.

"So you see, we need to get Tassore to Japazaw as soon as possible," she concluded breathlessly.

"I'm not sure he'll like it, miss," said the scout, but he swung Tassore over his shoulder and carried her into Werowocomoco.

When Pocahontas banged on the doorway of the House of Bones, there was a rustle and the mat was pulled slightly to one side. Japazaw peered out. The black paint around his eyes was smudged and one of his greased tufts of hair was awry.

"What is it?" he asked, yawning.

Pocahontas quickly explained.

"I know Tassore's only a slave," she finished, "but I feel terrible about what's happened. It was my fault – I ordered her into the forest."

"Well, she can't come in here," said Japazaw firmly. "The House of Bones is a sacred place. I won't have a slave defiling it."

Pocahontas was expecting this. Even she had never been inside this sacred place and she was a werowance's daughter. "Couldn't you treat her outside?" she pleaded.

Japazaw rolled his eyes.

"Put her down, but not too close."

Rawhunt laid Tassore on the ground just outside the doorway. She was sweating and the hideous gash now had a worrying greenish hue.

Japazaw examined the wound carefully before disappearing back into the House of Bones.

"I'd better go and tell the chief you're safe," said Rawhunt. "He's been worrying all night... And Namontack – our new hero – you should be on your way."

"Did you hear that?" whispered Namontack furiously once they were alone. "I told you." And he stormed off, leaving Pocahontas feeling terrible.

She wanted to chase after him to apologize and make things right, but she couldn't leave Tassore. Just then Japazaw emerged with a clay cup, a rattle, some dried herbs and a lump of suet. The priest circled Tassore three times, shaking the rattle and sprinkling her with droplets of sacred water. He then took a bunch of grey leaves, chewed them to a paste and spat them onto the cut.

"Dedicate these to Okeus," he said, handing Pocahontas a chunk of deer fat and a small pile of tobacco. "If she's to recover, the fever will drop by nightfall. Now get her away from here."

Once Pocahontas had settled Tassore in the slave yi-hakan, she rolled the sticky fat in the dried strands of tobacco and dropped it into the fire. The suet melted and the burning tobacco filled the room with its heady perfume.

"Please Okeus, let her get better," prayed Pocahontas. "And please make Namontack forgive me."

Okeus must have heard her pleas about Tassore, because by the afternoon her forehead was cooler and by the evening she was sleeping peacefully.

"If she gets worse again, wake me," Pocahontas instructed a slave boy.

By the time she returned to her own yi-hakan, only her sister Otta was awake.

"Where have you been?" she asked, sitting up on her elbows.

Pocahontas threw off her muddy dress and slipped gratefully under her deerskin rug.

"It's a long story," she said. "I'll tell you in the morning."

And then she drifted into a dreamless, exhausted
sleep.

POCAHONTAS opened her eyes slowly. The sun was high in the sky. She must have been sleeping for ages. She was about to get out of bed when Wassacan came in, looking disapproving.

"Ah, you're awake."

"How's Tassore?" Pocahontas asked immediately. "Have you heard?"

"She's still sleeping," said Wassacan through pursed lips. "She's better, but Japazaw says it'll be spring before she can walk again. Here's your breakfast."

She handed over a steaming bowl of corn porridge and a shell for a spoon.

Pocahontas ate ravenously. It was her first proper meal in two nights.

"Can I see her?" she asked when she'd scraped the bowl clean.

"Once you're dressed, but remember she's only a slave. No more visits after this one. It's not becoming for the daughter of a chief."

Pocahontas slipped out of bed. The shelter was, as usual, immaculate and there was no sign of the muddy clothes she'd dropped on the floor the previous evening.

"Wassacan, where's my dress?" she asked.

"It was covered with blood and grime. One of the slaves is washing it."

Suddenly, Pocahontas remembered the gold earring. If anyone found it it would be a disaster. Trying to keep her voice as casual as possible she asked, "There wasn't anything in the pocket was there? I'm sure I left a bead there."

Since the day Parahunt had given her the turquoise bead she'd carried it around with her.

"You did," said Wassacan, pointing at the shelf at the back of the yi-hakan. "It's over there."

"And there was nothing else?" asked Pocahontas.

"No."

Where's the earring? she thought, frantically trying to remember the last time she'd seen it. She was sure she'd shown it to Namontack in the clearing. *The forest... I must have dropped it there*, she decided. But how could she be sure?

"Get a move on," said Wassacan impatiently, interrupting her thoughts. "I want you helping your sisters by lunchtime and there's to be no more disappearing off."

Wassacan was true to her word. It was her job to oversee the girls and Chief Powhatan was not pleased that his favourite daughter had been lost in the woods. His firm instructions were that nothing like this was to happen again, so Pocahontas and her sisters were watched from dawn until dusk. It was stiflingly dull and did nothing to take Pocahontas's mind from her worries. She was haunted by the fear that one night the palefaces would appear, demanding gold from her. And then there was Namontack – and Tassore, who she could do little to help. If Wassacan even saw her gaze linger on Tassore as she limped across the town square, she would upbraid her.

Each night, as Pocahontas lay tossing in her narrow bunk, she dreamed of the cosy home she'd shared in Hatto. If only she could get back there, she was sure everything would be all right.

NAMONTACK was sitting on his haunches close to a fire, sharpening a hatchet with a flint. The night sky was clear and a full moon illuminated the frosty town.

"Namontack!" Pocahontas shouted, great clouds of steam tumbling from her mouth. She pulled her cloak closer, covering her fringed suede dress and pretty shell necklace. "Come quickly! Father wants you."

Namontack had arrived home from Jamestown late that afternoon and it was the first time Pocahontas had seen him since they'd carried Tassore back to Werowocomoco.

"Why?" he asked. His tone was cold, showing Pocahontas that he hadn't forgiven her.

"I don't know, but everybody's there," she answered quietly. "All except Chanco. He's late."

They crossed the square in awkward silence.

Despite the chilly night air, the lodge was close and warm. Its walls were lined with warriors and at the far end Chief Powhatan was sitting on a stack of deerskins, sucking a pottery pipe, with his daughters in an arc behind him. As Namontack and Pocahontas approached he exhaled a great cloud of wispy blue smoke.

"Daughter, fan me."

Obediently, Pocahontas crouched at his feet and began wafting feathers around.

"So," said Chief Powhatan, turning to Namontack, "you've been in Werowocomoco for almost a winter. I've had excellent reports from Rawhunt. He says you've done better than he ever thought possible for a boy your age."

Namontack's hunched shoulders relaxed.

"When you asked to take the Huskanaw at only twelve winters," continued the chief, "I thought it preposterous. But after these accounts, and of course your bravery with the bear..."

"The bear, sir?" stammered Namontack, a shadow passing over his face.

"The grizzly," said Chief Powhatan impatiently. "Many men would have turned and run, but you saved a favourite daughter." He patted Pocahontas's head affectionately. "So you'll be pleased to hear that I *will* allow you to join the Huskanaw this spring. In the meantime you'll stay here. Rawhunt will oversee any additional preparation he sees fit and I've instructed Parahunt to continue to provide your family with food until you are in a position to do so yourself."

Pocahontas was delighted. Perhaps now Namontack would forgive her after all.

"Sir, I am most honoured. Thank you," said Namontack, falling to his knees.

As he got up, a cold draught blew through the lodge. Chanco had arrived, dishevelled and dusted with snow.

"Brother, where have you been?" asked Chief Powhatan testily. "You've missed my ruling on Namontack's Huskanaw."

"I apologize," said Chanco, shaking the frost from his cloak. "But I have important news. It's about the palefaces."

Pocahontas felt herself tense. Even the mention of them made her nervous.

"What is it?" asked her father.

"A man with hair as red as a fox led a group of them up the Chickahominy River as far as Apokant."

Foxy hair, thought Pocahontas with dread. *Could Chanco be talking about John Smith?*

"One of my spies asked him what he was doing," continued her uncle, "as he speaks a little Algonquian."

It had to be him.

"He speaks our language?" said the chief, surprised. "What did he say?"

"He said his name is 'John Smith' and he was bird hunting. I was sure he was lying so I had him ambushed and brought to me."

"You did what?" exploded Chief Powhatan. "I specifically ordered you to stay away from them and certainly not to harm them. How dare you go against me?"

"Sir, I had to. I was worried he might reach the Massawomecks and form an alliance with them."

"What are you talking about?" interrupted Japazaw, who was sitting just to the left of the chief's stage. "The palefaces are not dangerous. Rawhunt reports they're dropping like flies. In just ten nights, thirteen died. At this rate they'll be gone by spring."

"They appear weak, but they have strong magic. This man showed me a little arrow that he calls a 'compass' that always points in the same direction whichever way he turns. And he can make objects speak. He made some marks on some thin white stuff he called 'paper' and asked that it be delivered to his fort by one of my runners. He told me that they would return with three swords and five tomahawks and that is exactly what happened."

"It must be a trick," said Japazaw dismissively.

"It was no trick," said Chanco. "I'm telling you there's evil among them and we must root it out."

The chief pursed his lips in frustration.

"Brother, you say they are a danger, Japazaw says they are not. How can I decide for myself?"

"I've brought him to Werowocomoco for that very reason," said Chanco with a flourish. "My men are holding him outside."

AT the news that John Smith was just outside, Pocahontas had a sudden rush of blood to her head that left her feeling dizzy.

"Pocahontas, call the guards and tell them to bring their weapons," ordered Chief Powhatan.

She staggered to her feet and returned moments later with forty of Rawhunt's men. Then, feeling a little better from the fresh air, she sat back down at her father's feet as the warriors lined up, creating a path for the stranger to walk down.

"Chanco, bring him in," instructed the chief.

The crowded meeting lodge waited in tense silence and then in walked the paleface. As soon as she saw his copper hair and intense turquoise eyes, Pocahontas recognised the man who had saved her. John Smith was dressed in a dirty white linen shirt and britches, and from his right ear dangled a lone gold hoop, the pair of the one he'd given her.

Pocahontas's heart sank. He would surely know her and then her secret visit to Jamestown would be discovered. *Calm down*, she told herself. Then she'd been a scruffy bedraggled wretch covered with scratches and mud. Now her fringed dress was clean and neat, and she had a string of delicate shells around her neck. *He'll never know me ... except for Keffgore's bracelet!* Quickly she pulled the copper band up her arm until it was hidden beneath her sleeve.

"Chanco, you say he speaks our language," said Chief Powhatan, never taking his eyes off the pale-faced man.

"A little, sir."

John Smith was now standing directly in front of Chief Powhatan and feet away from Pocahontas. He was so close, she got a whiff of his unpleasant smell. She cautiously stole a glance to see what her sisters made of him. Most of them were covering their noses and looking horrified. Only Otta was gazing at his golden earring. She seemed entranced by the trinket.

"All right Chanco, let's find out what he's up to," ordered Chief Powhatan. He turned to Smith. "Why are you on my land?"

Smith licked his lips nervously, but he spoke clearly and firmly.

"Boat here by..." And he began blowing and waving his arms.

"He means 'wind'," said Chanco.

"Wind," agreed Smith, nodding enthusiastically. "Me wait, more English come."

"Who are the 'English'?" asked Chief Powhatan.

"My people. They take me away."

"Sir, don't believe him," whispered Chanco. "They've built a fort. That's not the action of men about to leave. And why did I find him so far up the river?"

As Pocahontas listened to this exchange, she began to relax a little. John Smith hadn't noticed her and he hadn't mentioned the gold.

"If you don't intend to stay," continued Chief Powhatan, "why were you exploring the Chickahominy River?"

"Explore?" asked Smith, looking perplexed.

"Searching ... looking," Chanco added helpfully.

"Me look big sea."

"Don't be ridiculous," said Chief Powhatan. "The Great Sea is just south of your fort."

"No... Me look another sea."

"There is no other sea."

"There is. It called the Pacific. Other men tell me of it and me look. Me want see world," answered Smith in stumbling Algonquian.

"He's lying again," said Chanco. "You can see it in his eyes. He's up to something. With his ability to speak our language and the things he has to trade, he keeps Jamestown from starving. If we kill him, we kill them all. We should do it tonight."

Pocahontas gasped. This was not what she was expecting. Surely her father wouldn't agree, not after he'd said the palefaces mustn't be harmed. But to her dismay Chief Powhatan shrugged his shoulders and said wearily, "Perhaps you're right, Chanco. We have nothing to lose.

Japazaw, get the stones."

Not the stones! They were two large egg-shaped rocks used for bashing enemies' brains out. Smith *was* about to be killed... Pocahontas couldn't let that happen. She owed him her life. Just as two warriors pushed Smith to his knees, she leaped up shouting, "No! No! You can't kill him! You'll have to kill me first!"

"Pocahontas, what on earth are you doing? Move out of the way!" ordered Chief Powhatan furiously.

But Pocahontas held the disbelieving John Smith's head firmly in one arm, pushing Japazaw and his stones away with the other, determined to save him.

None of the guards dared lay a hand on the chief's daughter. They stood stunned, uncertain what to do. Only Chanco tried to pull her away, tugging painfully at her left shoulder. He pulled her cape to the ground, breaking her necklace. Pink and white shells scattered over the floor but still Pocahontas clung on to the pale-faced man cowering beneath her.

"Daughter, stop!" commanded her father, his menacing voice echoing around the lodge. "I won't have it."

Suddenly Pocahontas came to her senses. She wouldn't save Smith this way. What had she been thinking? All around people were gaping at her in disbelief. Namontack was gulping like a fish. Otta looked at her as if she were mad.

She stood up, pushing the astonished Smith behind her.

"Explain yourself!" said her father.

Pocahontas couldn't reveal she'd been to the fort. She couldn't say that she owed this man her life, not after the tales she'd already told.

"Well?" said Chief Powhatan, looking more and more irritated.

She knew she had to say something. Nervously she slipped her hand into her pocket and there she felt the smooth shiny bead that Parahunt had given her. The bead!

"If we kill all the palefaces, we won't get any more beads," she said, knowing it was ridiculous but unable to think of anything else.

"Beads?" asked her father as the spectators in the lodge tittered nervously.

This was getting worse and worse. It was embarrassing and hopeless. Her father must think her a complete idiot but there was no turning back now.

"Yes, beads," she answered, holding out the exquisite turquoise sphere. "Parahunt gave me this and he showed me a knife made from something they call 'iron' that can cut through a log like a shell runs through sand. This paleface could show us how to make them, but if we kill him we'll never learn."

She hardly knew what she was saying but, astonishingly, her father didn't look furious. Instead he turned to Chanco and said thoughtfully, "You said that Smith is valuable to the palefaces... That he's the only one keeping their fort going."

"Yes, brother."

"If he's that valuable, they will trade a lot for him. Perhaps I am being too hasty. Rawhunt says only forty foreigners are left. More die every night. Before long they'll all be gone and my daughter is right: before that happens we should learn all we can from them. Chanco, I want you to swap Smith for as much as we can get."

"But, sir, they're not to be trusted," protested Chanco. "They'll—"

"I've made up my mind," interrupted Chief Powhatan.

He turned to Smith, who was now back on his feet, his blue eyes darting this way and that.

"Smith, you will live."

The foreigner seemed to sway with relief. Pocahontas couldn't believe it. She'd saved his life.

"You will leave tomorrow for your fort with twelve of my men as an escort, do you understand?" continued Chief Powhatan.

"Yes," Smith mumbled.

"In return for this you will give me cannons, fire-sticks, hatchets, knives … and beads for my daughter. Do you agree?"

"Yes."

"And later you will show us how to make these things."

"Of course."

"Rawhunt, find him a bed for the night and then take him home first thing in the morning. And make sure he washes. He stinks."

Before he was led away, Smith turned to Pocahontas.

"Thank you," he mouthed and then his eyes flashed as he caught sight of the copper bangle that had slipped down her arm in the struggle with Chanco. In an instant Pocahontas was certain Smith knew who she was and she prayed he wouldn't betray her.

"All of you are dismissed," announced Chief Powhatan, "except for Pocahontas."

Once the lodge was empty, Chief Powhatan sat down heavily on his throne of skins and sighed.

"Pocahontas, I like you, but you are too headstrong."

"I'm sorry, Father, I..."

"Don't interrupt," said her father firmly. "I will forgive today's disobedience because you have been wise but if you embarrass me again, if you break any one of our rules, no matter how small, you will be punished. Do you understand?"

"Yes, sir," said Pocahontas, but secretly she knew she couldn't obey him. She was even with John Smith but she still needed to free Tassore.

THE next morning, Pocahontas joined the small crowd watching John Smith being led away from Werowocomoco by Rawhunt and a band of twelve warriors. As they dropped out of sight, Pocahontas was relieved. She hoped she would have nothing more to do with Smith or his pale-faced men – all they seemed to do was bring trouble.

She strolled back across the square and had just reached the daughters' yi-hakan when a young slave came running towards her.

"I've been looking all over for you," he exclaimed breathlessly. "You're to come straight to the chief and I'm warning you, he doesn't look happy."

Chief Powhatan's yi-hakan was next to the meeting lodge and was slightly larger than the rest, with a thick covering of sycamore bark. At the entrance were four guards, two on either side.

"You're expected," said one of the men gruffly as she approached.

Pocahontas went inside and was surprised to find Otta delicately pouring nut juice into a tortoiseshell cup while Namontack was sitting forlornly in the corner.

"Good day, Father," said Pocahontas, wondering what

was about to happen.

"Sit down over there," said Chief Powhatan coldly, and then he called out, "Guards, fetch the other one."

Moments later, Tassore was roughly pushed inside. She tumbled to the ground, her weak leg crumpling beneath her. Pocahontas was even more confused. What was going on?

"Father, what is wrong?" she asked.

"Why didn't you tell me you knew John Smith? Why didn't you tell me you'd been to Jamestown?"

"What do you mean?" asked Pocahontas, desperately playing for time. How could her father know?

"Do you deny it?"

Pocahontas didn't know what to say.

"And you, Namontack? What was your role, heh? And you, Tassore?"

Silence. Namontack looked petrified while Tassore just stared at the chief, her almond eyes brimming with hatred.

"Pocahontas, I'm sure you're the leader of this trio. Have you nothing to say?"

Pocahontas's mind was reeling. Smith must have betrayed her last night, but if she denied everything surely Chief Powhatan would believe her over a stranger.

"Father, I don't know what you're talking about," she said as resolutely as she could.

"Then how do you explain this?"

He opened his hand. There, glimmering in the firelight, was Smith's gold earring.

"Wasn't the foreigner wearing that last night?" asked Pocahontas

"No," said Chief Powhatan. "This is the one he gave you."

Pocahontas knew she was trapped. John Smith *had* told her father about her forbidden visit. There was nothing to do but confess.

"Father, I'm sorry," she stammered, not taking her eyes off the wretched gold hoop. "I should have told you, but—"

"When I ordered the tribe not to go to the palefaces' fort, I could not have been clearer," said her father dismissively, "and so I'm not interested in your excuses. You've lied once. Why should I listen to anything you say?"

Pocahontas had no answer, but it wasn't fair for either Namontack or Tassore to get blamed.

"Father, Namontack and Tassore are not responsible for what happened. I talked them into it."

"Be silent!" said Chief Powhatan, turning instead to the trembling Namontack. "Your Huskanaw is cancelled... Forever. You will never become a man. Until I decide how else to punish you, you are forbidden from leaving Werowocomoco. Now go."

Namontack got to his feet looking dazed. Pocahontas couldn't believe it. Poor Namontack, and his mother and five tiny sisters. What would become of them? If only she hadn't involved him. If only she hadn't been so insistent… But her father was still talking and things were getting worse.

"A slave that cannot be trusted," he said witheringly, "must be kept a prisoner. From now on, Tassore, you will not leave the confines of the slave hut. Pochins will make sure you do all your work there."

Pocahontas was horrified. Now it would be impossible for Tassore to get away.

"Father, no," she pleaded. "She doesn't deserve that."

"You've changed my mind once," said her father, "but you won't do it again. You must stay away from Tassore. I forbid you to go anywhere near her. Now leave. I can't bear to have you in my sight."

Otta jumped to her feet and led them to the door.

"I'm so sorry," she whispered to Pocahontas as she rolled up the mat.

Pocahontas stumbled out into the freezing square with only one thought in her head. It was those wretched palefaces. Ever since they'd arrived things had gone wrong.

"COME on," ordered Wassacan. "The palefaces are coming. Hurry up!"

Pocahontas was lying on her bunk with her back to the doorway, staring morosely at the wicker wall. It was late afternoon and the sun was low in the sky. She'd finished her chores and was sheltering in the yi-hakan, partly from the freezing temperatures and the disapproving looks that followed her wherever she went, but also because the palefaces, and particularly John Smith, were the last people she wanted to see.

"Do I have to?" said Pocahontas without turning over. "Father won't want me there."

Since the night, seven evenings ago, when John Smith had been freed, he'd sent Chief Powhatan beads, hatchets and spades, and now a message: the palefaces were coming to pay homage to the great chief.

"Your father won't see you," said Wassacan. "He's in the meeting lodge, but it'll look strange if one of his daughters is missing. If you hide away, everyone will think you're a coward."

Pocahontas knew Wassacan was right. She *was* hiding and she couldn't do it forever, so she pulled out a bearskin cape, tied it over her suede dress, and went out into the freezing night.

Pocahontas had never seen the square so crowded. The ground was covered with muddy slush and the temperature was falling fast but that hadn't deterred a single Powhatan. Everyone wanted to see the strange pale men. Wrapped up in furs, moccasins and leggings, people jostled for the places with the best view. Fathers lifted children onto their shoulders; mothers took babies out of their papooses and held them aloft.

Lined up outside the entrance to the meeting lodge were the seven wives. They were all dressed in their finest dresses with jaunty feathers stuck in their hair. Otta was there too, standing closest to the doorway. Her face sparkled with silver ore and her fringed dress was covered in pearls.

"The palefaces have landed! Move back!" shouted Rawhunt, organizing a pathway through the crowd.

A moment later, twenty palefaces marched into the muddy square, with the last person Pocahontas wanted to see leading the way – John Smith. He was dressed in dark brown trousers, knee-high leather boots with shiny buckles, a linen shirt and a heavy wool coat.

"Look at their hair!" commented an elderly woman.

"And their beards," said another.

"They look half dead to me," said a third. "They're skin and bone."

Chanco and Japazaw emerged from the meeting

lodge. Chanco wore only a loincloth and his snow-white mantle whereas Japazaw was dressed in his finest regalia – a crown of parakeet feathers and a black and white coat sewn from striped raccoon tails. His stuffed blackbird swung above his ear.

John Smith bowed low.

"Where chief?" he asked.

"He's waiting for you inside," explained Japazaw. "Follow me."

"No, only two of my men at one time," said Smith.

"He's nervous we'll ambush them," Pocahontas heard someone mutter.

"Chief Powhatan wants to welcome *all* of you," explained the priest patiently.

"Two," said Smith firmly, holding up two fingers. Then he turned and said something incomprehensible, and a nervous-looking boy of around fifteen winters stepped out from among the band of palefaces. He was tall and lanky, with a long nose, wide green eyes and a thin, scraggy neck. Unlike the others, his clothes were patched, his britches had a rip at the knee and his feet were bare.

Japazaw shrugged his shoulders. "As you wish." He and Chanco led Smith and the boy into the meeting lodge, followed by Otta and the wives.

Nobody in the square moved. The Powhatans couldn't take their eyes off the band of sickly, strange men standing only feet away. Half of Pocahontas wanted to get away but she was too curious to leave. *What on earth could be going on inside the meeting lodge?* she thought. *What trick could Smith be playing?*

Just as the sun sank below the walls of Werowocomoco, Chief Powhatan emerged from the lodge with John Smith and the gangly boy at his side.

"Otta, fetch Namontack," he ordered.

Oh no! thought Pocahontas. If her father was calling for Namontack, this must be bad.

Namontack made his way through the crowd, looking downcast and unhappy.

"As a sign of friendship and to help us learn more from the palefaces," announced Chief Powhatan, "John Smith has given me a boy. His name is Tom Savage." He pronounced the unfamiliar name slowly and precisely, looking at Smith to make sure he'd got it right. "In return," he continued, "he's asked for a boy to take to his own village so that the palefaces can learn our language. I've decided to send Namontack. He will leave tonight."

Pocahontas felt as though she'd been punched in the stomach. Because of her, Namontack was condemned to live in that awful starving fort.

FRANTICALLY Pocahontas pushed through the jostling crowd. She was desperate to get away from the teeming square and her cruel father. The rest of the town was deserted. She wandered past a couple of homes and found herself near the slave quarters.

"Who's that?" said a voice with a southern accent.

Pocahontas turned around sharply. Tassore was sitting in the freezing shadows, her ankle tied so tightly to a wooden stake that it was red and swollen.

Pocahontas couldn't bear it any longer. For the first time in many moons, she sank to the ground and wept, not caring that her father had forbidden her from being anywhere near Tassore.

"What's wrong?" asked the slave, inching her way as close to Pocahontas as her shackle would allow.

"It's all my fault," she sobbed. "Father's just exiled Namontack to Jamestown. If it wasn't for me, he would be doing his Huskanaw and you'd be free."

"What's happened to me isn't your fault," said Tassore. "I was a slave and I chose to run away."

"Well, what about Namontack?" Pocahontas mumbled into her knees.

"You were only trying to help me. Namontack knows that."

"That doesn't help him though, does it?" said Pocahontas. "He'll starve in Jamestown. They've no food. You saw what it was like."

Tassore looked troubled.

"I'm sorry, you have enough worries," said Pocahontas, suddenly realizing that Namontack's woes were the last thing Tassore needed to hear.

"Don't worry," said the slave and then she added tentatively, as if she hadn't quite made up her mind about something, "is there any chance you could get back to Jamestown?"

"Why?" asked Pocahontas.

"Because... Because... Because I know where there's food... Enough to feed all of them."

Pocahontas lifted her head from her knees.

"What do you mean?"

Tassore answered quietly. "I've never told anyone before; the whole tribe was sworn to secrecy."

"About what?"

Tassore glanced around her and then whispered, "The village of Skicoak was so close to the water, we built a second House of Bones high in the hills. It was mainly a place to store food, to stop it from getting damp and spoiling, but our chief decided not to tell your father. He knew Chief Powhatan would only ask for a larger tribute. The place is in the woods just above the Tussan Falls.

If you look carefully, you'll find a trail behind a granite boulder at the top of the waterfall." She paused again. "You won't tell anyone else about this, will you?"

"Of course not," said Pocahontas, "but why are you telling me?"

"Use those stores to feed Namontack."

"I can't do that," protested Pocahontas. "They belong to your tribe."

"My tribe is gone," said Tassore sadly. "Take what you need. I want you to. It will be my way of repaying Namontack for all he did for me."

Suddenly they heard voices nearby.

"Go! Quickly!" said Tassore. "If your father discovers us we'll both be punished."

Pocahontas was instantly on her feet. Now at least she had something to think about, something that could help Namontack.

Nights passed and infuriatingly Pocahontas never had a moment to herself. On her fathers' orders Wassacan kept her busy from dawn until dusk scraping hides, spinning twine and weaving mats. But all the time Pocahontas was thinking of Namontack and how she must find a way to get to the Chesepiock stores.

One morning as the sisters emerged shivering from the Mattaponi River after their daily swim, Wassacan announced, "Today you're all to collect firewood, except Pocahontas. I have something special for her to do."

She said "special" with an emphasis that made Pocahontas's heart sink. "What is it?" she asked warily.

"The tuckahoe roots will soon be ready. Every five nights you will visit the creeks and bring back samples from each one for me to see if they're ripe. You'll start today."

This was a new humiliation; everyone knew this was a job for a slave. Grubbing around in the marshes was unpleasant but also dangerous. In spring, storms came quickly, whipping up waves that could easily capsize a canoe.

"Wassacan, surely Father can't have agreed to this," said Amonsens, the youngest half-sister.

"Actually, these are Chief Powhatan's instructions."

So now Pocahontas knew just how little her father cared for her. One look at her sisters told her they knew too. Otta didn't even meet her eye.

"Take that canoe," said Wassacan, pointing to a boat moored nearby. "Start with Chuckatuck Creek and then move on to the others. And don't mess around. I want you back by noon."

Pocahontas frowned. She had to get to Jamestown and instead she was banished to the muddy waterways when everyone knew the roots weren't ready yet. *But maybe,* she suddenly thought, *this could be just what I need.*

She glanced at the sky. The sun was still low. She had almost the whole morning to herself... And she'd have it again in five nights' time and again five nights after that.

Somehow, she had to use this unexpected freedom and she had the beginnings of an idea how.

POCAHONTAS paddled slowly round the first bend in the Mattaponi River and then, when she was sure she was out of sight, she sped up, tugging at the water with all her might until she spotted Chuckatuck Creek. It was a large expanse of water surrounded by pine and oak trees. On the far side was a marsh where herons and egrets were wading. She steered the canoe that way and soon spotted the arrowhead-shaped leaves of the starchy, nutritious tuckahoe plants. Last summer's crop of corn was running low and the autumn's nuts were almost exhausted. In a couple of moons, the potato-like roots of the tuckahoe plant would be the Powhatan's main source of food.

Her boat ran aground and Pocahontas clambered out, her feet sinking into the sticky mud. She bent down, dug her fingers into the sludge, grabbed the nearest root and pulled hard. After several tugs, it came up with a satisfying *plop*. She washed it in the freezing waters and examined it carefully. *Not nearly swollen enough*, she thought. *Good.* There were more creeks to go to, but no time if she was to have a chance of reaching the Tussan Falls, so Pocahontas grabbed some more roots, from the weediest, least ripe plants she could find, threw them into the boat and then paddled back to the river.

She hid the canoe in a large clump of reeds and then headed off into the forest, jogging at a fast and steady pace.

There was a thin layer of cloud overhead and a slight breeze – perfect weather for running – and she made good progress. By mid-morning, she was standing at the top of the narrow gorge above the falls. Tassore had said Skicoak's stores were kept in a House of Bones built in a hollow behind a large granite boulder. She looked around. There, on the other side of the waterfall, was a grey slab of rock. *That must be it*, she thought excitedly.

Below her the stream narrowed, rushing through fallen rocks before tumbling down into the valley below. The boulders were slippery with spray and covered with moss but they were just close enough to jump from one to the next. Pocahontas leapt nimbly across, not daring to look down. On the far side, the grass was uneven – a thin strip shorter and more worn than the rest. *An overgrown path. This must be the way.* She hurried into the trees. Here and there she found traces of footprints - she must be getting nearer. The forest floor inclined steeply. She scrambled up the slope, her feet slipping on the crumbly earth, and there below her she saw just what she'd been looking for – a clearing and in its centre the Chesepiocks' House of Bones.

Cautiously, she climbed down the side of the mound.

The abandoned structure was made from saplings covered with woven reed mats. Several mats had come loose and were mouldy in patches, and one corner was badly gnawed.

She rolled up the entrance mat and slipped inside. It was musty and gloomy, lit only by a shaft of dappled light streaming through a small smoke-hole in the ceiling. Everything was just as it must have been the day the Chesepiocks were attacked. The walls were hung with masks, tomahawks and bones, and a beautiful cape, woven from black and white turkey feathers, hung on its hook waiting for its owner to return. The place sent a shiver down Pocahontas's spine. She couldn't wait to get away, but first she must see whether the corn had escaped the attention of the raccoons, squirrels and muskrats that inhabited the woods.

She hurriedly crossed to the second room and then paused at the deerskin mat that covered the doorway. As the daughter of Chief Powhatan, she had occasionally been allowed to enter the first room of the small House of Bones in Hatto, but never the second. That was strictly for the tribe's chief and priest. It was a holy place, used to store statues of gods, pearls, copper, beautiful furs, medicines, precious talismans and food.

She took a deep breath, pulled the soft pelt to one side — and screamed. A hideous statue of Okeus blocked the way. It was carved from wood, had bulging eyes and thick leering lips, and looked as if it were about to pounce.

Calm down, she told herself as she squeezed past the grotesque figure and into a dark chamber with a monstrous carving in each corner: a bear, cougar, wolf and a huge swooping raven, all with white luminous shell eyes. The walls were lined with shelves stacked high with covered baskets on one side and large pottery urns on the other, and at the far end of the room was a raised platform with six long lumps covered with bearskins and strings of pearl. *What could they be?* Pocahontas's heart began to race. The Chesepiocks must have chosen to keep the tribe's most sacred objects here... The dried-out bodies of ancient chiefs.

Trying not to look at the unnerving platform, she hurriedly crossed over to the nearest shelf and lifted off the lid of a basket. Pungent tobacco. She searched the next ... shells ... and the next ... pearls. This wasn't what she wanted; it was food she was after. *Where would that be kept? The pottery urns!* They would keep predators out. But as she reached them, there was a clattering sound. Somehow, a pearl necklace had slipped off a chief and then Pocahontas realized with horror that one of the bodies was moving.

POCAHONTAS stared at the platform. There it was again. The lump on the far side definitely shifted ever so slightly to the left. *What was going on? How could a corpse move?* Pocahontas's heart was pumping and her breath was shallow and fast. *I've got to get out of here*, she thought, but in the gloom she crashed straight into the statue of Okeus. She screamed as its wooden arm clattered to the ground. The statue was sacred. She ought to mend it, but how could she stay in the same place as that thing behind her? She glanced over her shoulder. The lump was definitely alive. It was sitting up, its bearskin cover slipping from it. Pocahontas didn't want to know what was underneath. Desperately she tucked the arm of Okeus back into its sleeve but her hands were shaking too much and it fell to the floor once more. The thing would be across the room in moments. *Leave,* she told herself, *before it catches you!* She glanced behind her one last time, expecting to see a monster, but it wasn't a fiend or ogre. Astonishingly, standing on the far side of the platform was a girl, looking as terrified as she was.

"Don't hurt me," she pleaded.

Pocahontas was too stunned to respond.

"What are you doing here?" The girl's voice sounded strangely familiar.

"Looking for food," Pocahontas managed to mumble.

"But you're not a Chesepiock, are you?"

"No."

"Then how do you know about this place?" Again, there was something about the girl's clipped southern accent that she recognized.

Pocahontas took a step closer. The girl was slim, with two plaits, a pointed nose and a narrow face ornately tattooed. It was Tassore! But how could she be here? Was this one of Okeus's cruel tricks?

The girl clambered off the platform. She had Tassore's almond-shaped brown eyes and those distinctive blue fish on her cheeks.

"Tassore?" asked Pocahontas, thoroughly confused. "How did you get here?"

The girl was equally perplexed.

"Not Tassore," she said. "Suckahanna."

"Suckahanna?"

And then Pocahontas remembered: Tassore had a twin.

"Are you Tassore's sister?" she asked, only half believing it could be possible.

The girl nodded slowly.

"She thought you'd been killed."

"Is she alive?"

"Yes. She's in Werowocomoco."

With that Suckahanna sank to the ground. "I've prayed

and prayed for somebody to find me," she said between great gulping sobs. "It's been so lonely here all by myself."

"How did you survive?" asked Pocahontas, crouching down and putting her arm around the distraught girl. "How did you escape the warriors?"

Suckahanna wiped the tears from her cheeks.

"I was on the beach hunting oysters when they attacked. I was so scared I hid behind a rock. All afternoon I heard the most terrible cries and then the warriors left and it was all quiet. It wasn't until sunset that I had the courage to go back to Skicoak and I'll never forget what I saw. There were bodies everywhere, hacked to pieces. I couldn't even recognize some of them but once I was certain mother and father had been killed I ran away and I've never been back."

"What did you do?"

"I couldn't risk going to another tribe, not after I'd seen warriors murder my people, so I hid here in the House of Bones. But it's been so lonely, especially at night when the wolves howl in the woods." And then she looked up eagerly. "But now I won't be on my own, not if Tassore's alive. Can you take me to her?"

"No," said Pocahontas, and with a heavy heart she explained why.

"You mean she can't ever leave Werowocomoco?" asked Suckahanna.

"She will. I'm going to help her get away when her leg is healed, but that won't be for several moons."

"So why did you come here today?"

Pocahontas told her who she was and about the ill-fated trip to Jamestown and her plans to feed Namontack.

"I've seen those pale men in the forest," said Suckahanna, her eyes wide with fear. "I daren't go near them but there is food to spare and if Tassore wants you to have it, you can."

"Thank you," said Pocahontas. "But the problem is getting it to Namontack. You see, I don't have much time."

"I could help."

Pocahontas shook her head. It wasn't fair to send Suckahanna to that terrible fort.

"There must be something," persisted the girl. "It would be my way of repaying you for freeing my sister."

And then Pocahontas remembered the roots. If Suckahanna collected the tuckahoes for her, it would give her time to get to Jamestown and back.

"Do you know your way to the Chuckatuck Creek off the Mattaponi River?" she asked.

"Yes."

"Then you *can* help. Meet me by its entrance in five nights' time. I'll be there, just after dawn."

26

AS the sun rose, Pocahontas paddled into the first creek. She knew she was early but she wanted to be ready to go as soon as Suckahanna arrived.

Five nights ago, on her return to Werowocomoco, Wassacan had inspected the roots suspiciously and asked why it had taken her so long to collect such a paltry bundle. Pocahontas said that the tides had been against her and that she needed to start earlier and so here she was, waiting in the grey morning light.

The river was cold and still, and the air chilly. Pocahontas was wearing nothing but bear grease and leggings. She would be running for most of the morning and didn't want heavy clothes to slow her down, but now that she wasn't moving she began to shiver.

"Pocahontas!"

It was Suckahanna. Pocahontas paddled over to the bank.

"Are you sure you know all the creeks?" she asked as she moored the canoe.

"Yes."

"Remember, pull a root from each one – the least ripe you can find – and I'll meet you here at midday. Do you understand?"

"Yes, and don't worry. I'll collect all the tuckahoes you need."

By the time Pocahontas reached the secret House of Bones, she was dripping with sweat and breathless but relieved. She was over halfway to Jamestown. The sun was not too high in the sky. She had time.

Suckahanna had left a large basket full of corn by the entrance. *Good,* she thought. She wouldn't have to go back into that creepy place. She picked it up. It was too heavy to run with, but by balancing it on her head she made good progress down the steep path to Jamestown and was soon at the edge of the clearing. Here she tidied herself as best she could and stepped out into the meadow.

She was around twenty yards from the fort when a wooden gate swung open and a skinny man with a bulbous red nose emerged pointing a fire-stick.

"Smith," she said, trying to remember the strange pronunciation of the foxy-haired paleface's name. "John Smith."

The skinny man called over his shoulder and moments later Smith was standing in the doorway, his legs apart and his arms folded over his chest. As soon as she saw him, Pocahontas realized how much she loathed him. He repulsed her, with his hairy face and dirty fingernails, but more than that, he'd betrayed her to her father just when she'd saved him. But she must let none of this show if her plan was to work, so she forced herself to smile.

"So it's you again," he said. "Why are you here?"

Pocahontas noticed immediately how his Algonquian had improved. It was heavily accented, but much clearer.

"I want to see Namontack."

"Why?"

"I have food for him," she said, picking up a handful of corn, and letting the grains run tantalizingly through her fingers. "Then he will be less of a burden to you."

Smith's blue eyes never left the corn.

"Did your father send you?"

"He doesn't know I'm here, and if he finds out, I won't come again."

John Smith studied her carefully.

"Namontack is not the only one who needs food," he said at last. "We're all hungry. Why should he alone eat?"

Pocahontas had thought he might say this, but all those urns in the Chesepiock House of Bones were brimming with enough corn to feed a village so she answered, "Then I'll bring more, enough to feed you all."

"A child can't feed fifty men."

"I can and I'll tell you how, but only after I've seen Namontack."

They walked in silence across a muddy square towards a small hut on the far side of the fort. It was built from logs, with a thatched roof and four openings to let in light. Pocahontas was just wondering why the palefaces hadn't included an entrance when Smith pulled a metal handle and a wooden door magically swung open.

The room was furnished quite differently from any Pocahontas had seen before. It had whitewashed walls, a stone fireplace and chimney with a large iron cooking pot, and an oak dresser covered in beautiful white and blue plates, glasses and pewter tankards. In the middle was a sturdy-looking table and two wooden chairs. Sitting on the one closest to the fire was a boy with his back to her.

"You have a visitor," said Smith.

The boy turned around. Pocahontas was amazed. It was Namontack, but dressed as she had never seen him before. Rather than a loincloth, he was wearing brown knee-length trousers and a grey linen shirt, and his hair was almost an inch long. He looked just like a paleface.

"Pocahontas!" said Namontack, leaping out of his seat. "I can't believe it's you!"

Pocahontas was relieved. At least he was no longer angry with her.

"I'll be back soon," said John Smith.

"What are you doing here?" exclaimed Namontack as soon as they were alone.

"I want to make things up to you. I'm going to make sure you don't starve."

"How?"

Pocahontas explained about the Chesepiocks' secret supplies.

"I'm going to bring them here, but only if you get your fair share. Do you think I can trust John Smith to do that?"

Namontack sat back by the fire, looking thoughtful. "As long as he's getting something from the bargain, he should keep his side but make sure you ask to see me each time you come; then you'll know."

"What's he like? How should I approach him?"

"He's a warrior. He fought in wars in a place he calls 'Europe', and he speaks many languages. That's why he's learned ours so quickly. But he's also practical; he's now the chief of Jamestown. The place would fall apart without him."

This surprised Pocahontas. "Why, what do the others do?"

"Nothing. They don't hunt or fish or prepare fields for spring. They just sit around getting weaker and weaker."

"What do they live off?"

"Supplies they brought with them from home, but they're running out. Smith tries to persuade them to learn from us and live off the land but most of them won't. They say they're too grand to work."

"But even my father hunts and he's the grandest chief there is."

"I know," said Namontack. "I don't understand it, but that's the reason there's not enough food. If it wasn't for the corn they sometimes manage to trade for metal and beads, they'd be starving. As it is, there's not much. All I get each day is a bowl of porridge and that's going to run out soon. And some of the tribes have been stealing hammers, knives and even fire-sticks from the fort so the palefaces haven't even got much left to trade."

Just then, before Pocahontas had a chance to ask any more questions, John Smith returned.

"You've had your time," he said gruffly. "Pocahontas, what's your proposal?"

Pocahontas looked him straight in the eye.

"I'll bring two baskets of corn every fifth night and I'll do that until summer, when the deer return and the bay will be teeming with fish."

"And why would you do that?" asked Smith. "It can't be for the love of us English."

"No, certainly not," said Pocahontas haughtily. "I'm doing it to save Namontack. I'll only feed Jamestown if he gets his share."

"Then I'd be mad not to agree," said Smith.

Even though it was the answer Pocahontas was expecting, she was still relieved. She had no desire to help John Smith or his sickly men, but it was the only way to save her friend.

"Good. Now, I must go," she said. "Will you let Namontack accompany me a little way?"

"To the gate and no further," said Smith.

They walked across the main square. It was a dismal place, dotted with thatched houses and skinny exhausted-looking men.

"Thank you for trying to help," said Namontack as they approached the gate, "but once Smith is fluent in Algonquian he'll tire of me and then who knows what he'll do. One thing I'm certain of, he's no friend of ours. All he wants is for Jamestown to survive and he'll use anyone – his men or us – to achieve that."

Pocahontas felt awful. Thanks to her Namontack was stuck in Jamestown and, despite her best efforts, he was running out of time.

THIS morning would be her twelfth trip to Jamestown, Pocahontas calculated, as she pulled on her moccasins and tied leggings around her calves.

So far, her luck had held. Suckahanna was always waiting at the creek and was excellent at collecting roots, Namontack was getting enough to eat and Tassore's leg was healing well.

She slipped quietly out of the yi-hakan. The sky was grey, with a thick layer of cloud, and it was drizzling. By the time she arrived at the entrance to Chuckatuck Creek the drizzle had turned to rain. Suckahanna was sitting close to the river bank, sheltering under the boughs of a large oak tree.

"I'll see you at noon," said Pocahontas, passing over the canoe. "What a miserable day."

By the time Pocahontas reached Jamestown, it was raining hard and she was sopping wet and cold. The gate swung open and, as usual, there was John Smith waiting for her, a wide-brimmed hat and a black cape protecting him from the downpour.

"Let me see Namontack," said Pocahontas curtly once she'd handed over the precious grain.

"You'd better make the most of it. This will be the last time for a while."

Pocahontas spun around and stared at him.

"What are you talking about?" she said.

"He's sailing for England on today's tide."

"Why?"

"A boat has come to take the sicker men home and the captain's agreed to take Namontack too. In London he'll be an exotic specimen. He'll be paraded around the town. I'm hoping it will make other men curious enough to make the journey here. Jamestown needs more people."

"You can't take him away," protested Pocahontas.

"Yes I can. He was given to me in a fair exchange."

"But *we* had an agreement!"

"And I'm not breaking it." Smith smiled coldly. "He will still be fed."

"I won't know that. If you do this, I won't bring any more corn to Jamestown."

"Oh, I think you will," said Smith with a conviction that unnerved Pocahontas. "Otherwise, I'll let your father know exactly what you've been up to. Now, if you want to see your precious Namontack, you'd better hurry. He's in one of the cabins of the *John & Francis*."

Pocahontas ran across the main square to a gate that led to a small vegetable patch and beyond that the bay. Two boats were moored next to a spindly wooden quay, both creaking and pitching in the squally swell. The smaller one, the *Discovery*, had been there ever since the palefaces arrived but it had been joined by a much larger vessel. This had three great towering masts, dangling ropes and great white sails that flapped in the blustery wind. Its stern was painted with jaunty red and white checks and at its bow was the carved figure of a buxom woman with bright yellow hair, scarlet lips and blue eyes staring glassily out to sea.

On the shore several men were throwing the last couple of boxes and barrels to sailors on deck and as Pocahontas climbed the gangplank one of them pointed to a cabin at the back.

"Namontack, are you there?" she asked, pushing open the cabin door.

She found herself in a small, cramped room lit by a swaying lamp that hung from a hook in the ceiling. On one side of the room was a narrow bunk bed and on the other an oak table covered with bits of paper with pictures on and strange shiny objects. Namontack was sitting on a bench, his ankle manacled with a thick metal chain.

Pocahontas tugged at the shackle.

"It's useless," said Namontack miserably. "You need an iron thing they call a 'key'. It's the only thing that will release it."

"But I've got to get you out of here," said Pocahontas. "They can't take you away."

"You can't stop them. They haven't given up on discovering gold. They think if they bring back more men, they'll find it."

"Will you come back with them?"

"I hope so," Namontack answered forlornly. "My family need me. I can now understand most of what the palefaces say. Last night, Smith begged his stronger men to stay with him until we return, and they've agreed, as long as the food doesn't run out. If that happens, they will leave on the last boat they have here, the *Discovery*."

So Smith *did* have her trapped. In order for Namontack to return, Jamestown must keep going and for that to happen the fort must have food and she was its main supplier. Once more she rued the day that she'd saved John Smith's life. All he'd done was manipulate and betray her. Well, she'd feed his wretched Jamestown until Namontack's return and then she really would have nothing more to do with him.

28

AS Pocahontas left Jamestown, she took one last lingering look over her shoulder. Dark clouds were skidding across the sky but through the torrential rain she could just about make out the *John & Francis*. Her great white sails were billowing in the wind and she had already reached the far side of the bay, sailing out towards the Great Sea, taking Namontack with her. Pocahontas wondered if she'd ever see him again. When a paleface ship left, it was many moons before it returned. Anything could happen between now and then.

Directly above her there was a sudden flash of lightning followed by a crash of thunder. All around branches were swaying, and leaves and twigs were skittering across the sodden ground. A branch came thudding down only a few feet away. Pocahontas was cold; her hair was drenched, sticking in clumps to her bare back, and her moccasins and leggings were waterlogged and heavy. There was nothing for it. She must run to warm up and get back to Suckahanna. Suckahanna! In this gale the creeks would be treacherous! Why hadn't she warned her to abandon the search for the tuckahoes if the weather got bad? She had to get there as soon as she could.

When Pocahontas arrived at the entrance to the Chuckatuck Creek, exhausted and panting for breath, there was no sign of Suckahanna or her canoe. *Could she have sheltered in one of the inlets?* It would be madness to search. The marsh was divided up by hundreds of streams, and without a boat it was impossible. *No, the most sensible thing,* she told herself, *is to wait here until she comes back.*

The winds lessened and the sky was no longer a threatening grey, but there was still no sign of Suckahanna. Pocahontas sat at the water's edge, rubbing her arms and legs to keep warm and trying not to worry, but she couldn't help herself. Suckahanna had never been late before.

Pocahontas glanced up at the sky, estimating where the sun was, trying to keep some track of time. It was roughly her hands' width away from midday. She tried to distract herself by walking along the bank to a fish trap made from saplings and reeds where shad and herring were darting this way and that. She came back to the creek and couldn't resist checking once more. Now the sun was several hands after noon. Something must have gone wrong. And then she heard a splashing noise. A boat was coming, not from the direction of the Chuckatuck Creek but from the Mattaponi River. Quickly, she ducked behind a clump of reeds.

"Pocahontas!" Somebody – not Suckahanna – was shouting. "Are you there?"

Someone was looking for her now that the storm had cleared. It was the last thing she needed. With no canoe and no roots, how could she possibly explain what was going on?

29

"IS there anybody here?"

Suddenly Pocahontas recognized the voice. Otta! There, across the freezing black water, was her sister. Warmly wrapped in a thick fur, she was steering a canoe into the mouth of the creek.

A boat! Otta could help me find Suckahanna, thought Pocahontas. But could she trust her? Otta had been sympathetic when Chief Powhatan accused her over the earring. Just as Pocahontas made up her mind to chance it, the boat drifted closer, caught the breeze and swung to the left, and she saw that Otta wasn't alone. Her little half-sister Amonsens was sitting behind her, shivering in leggings without so much as a tunic to keep her warm. Pocahontas quickly crouched down behind the reeds.

"Pocahontas!" shouted Otta and then she said, "Amonsens, I give up. Let's go home."

In the still, cold air Pocahontas was surprised to find that even though Otta was talking quietly, she could hear every word.

"You promised you'd help me find her," replied Amonsens curtly. "At least let's search the first creek."

"Forget it," said Otta. "It's too dangerous."

"Then why tell Father to send Pocahontas here?"

"I don't know what you're talking about," said Otta sharply.

"I think you do." Amonsens spoke firmly and deliberately, most unlike her usual timid self. "That day Father confronted Pocahontas about the gold earring, Wassacan sent me to fetch a fur. I'd never been to the long-house by myself and was scared so I crept in. You were there with Father. You didn't notice me but I heard you say Pocahontas hadn't been punished enough for lying and that being sent to the creeks might bring her down a peg or two. And now look what's happened. She's lost in the storm and it's all your fault. Since the day she arrived, you've wanted her out of the way and now you've got your wish."

"She had it coming," Otta said defensively. "If I hadn't found the earring, Father would never have known what she was up to."

So it wasn't John Smith who betrayed me, it was Otta! thought Pocahontas. And she remembered the night she'd come back from Jamestown. Only Otta had been awake. Her sister must have searched her pockets when she'd fallen asleep.

"Don't pretend you did this for the tribe," said Amonsens. "You did it for you – to be Father's favourite again."

"How dare you talk to me like that!" screamed Otta, and without warning she stood up and lunged at her sister.

Through the reeds Pocahontas could see the canoe rocking alarmingly as it drifted towards the middle of the creek. *If they're not careful, that boat's going to capsize*, she thought. And then, quick as a flash, she realized how useful that would be. She had to make sure it happened.

She untied her moccasins and leggings, and slipped into the water. Taking one last look at her fighting sisters, she took several deep breaths and then dived deep below the surface of the water. By the time she'd swum halfway to the canoe, she was gasping for air but she couldn't risk coming up, so she willed herself to keep going. Her lungs were screaming but now she could see the shadow of the boat, looming only a few feet above her. *Hold on! Not long to go!* she told herself. She was directly under the canoe. She swam up, grabbed the side and yanked it as hard as she could.

There was a splash as her two half-sisters tumbled into the bitterly cold creek. Pocahontas filled her lungs and then swam to the end of the canoe and cautiously peeked around. There was Otta, thrashing around in the water in her bedraggled fur with Amonsens just beyond her. Both girls were spluttering and splashing. They were still far too shocked to notice what was going on around them, so Pocahontas quickly flipped the boat over until it was fully capsized.

Now for the trickiest part, she thought, and dived once more. Above her, two dark figures were moving this way and that. She had to be sure she had the right one...

Surely that was Otta's matted pelt cloak so those must be Amonsens's leggings. Pocahontas grabbed her sister's tiny ankle and pulled. Amonsens kicked hard but using all her strength, Pocahontas dragged her downwards, away from Otta and towards the upturned canoe. Only when they were hovering just below it did she let go and they both bobbed up into the pitch-black hull.

"Don't make a sound. It's me!" she whispered as her sister broke the surface gasping for breath.

"Pocahontas!" spluttered Amonsens in the gloom of the capsized boat.

"Be quiet or Otta will find us!"

They could hear Otta's splashes and frightened calls. Pocahontas knew she ought to feel sorry for her half-sister, swimming around in the creek terrified, but she couldn't, not now she knew what Otta had done.

"She thinks I've drowned," said Amonsens.

"Good," said Pocahontas. "Then she'll go for help."

"But shouldn't we tell her we're here?"

Pocahontas's eyes were getting used to the darkness and she could see Amonsens looked panicked.

"No. We're going to search the creeks."

"Why?" asked Amonsens, her voice squeaking with cold.

It was a question Pocahontas couldn't answer. She'd got too many people into trouble already and wanted to involve Amonsens as little as possible.

"It's best if all you know is that I'm looking for a girl

called Suckahanna. But believe me, I wouldn't ask you to help me if it wasn't important."

"All right, but we don't have much time," said Amonsens. "It can't be long before Otta returns with help."

If they hadn't been treading water in a freezing creek, Pocahontas would have hugged Amonsens. Now, at least, she had a chance of finding Suckahanna.

30

BY the time Otta's cries had faded into the distance, Pocahontas and Amonsens's legs were numb and their teeth chattering.

"She's swum away," whispered Pocahontas. "She must have reached the shore."

"Good, because I can't stand it any more," said Amonsens.

Both girls ducked under the water and emerged clinging to the side of the canoe. Warily they looked around. There was no sign of their sister.

"Let's get paddling," said Pocahontas. "It'll warm us up."

Together they flipped over the boat, pulled themselves into it and began rowing towards the first creek. "Suckahanna!" Pocahontas called at the top of her voice. Her cry echoed eerily around the silent creek. She shouted again and again, but there was no reply. They paddled into the second creek and then the third but still nothing. The fourth creek, wider and more desolate, was ringed by a thick forest of pine trees.

"Hold on, what's that?" asked Amonsens, pointing to the far side of the inlet. There was something among the reeds and tuckahoe stems.

The two girls paddled over furiously. It was a capsized canoe! They ran their boat aground, jumped out and waded through the mud to the stricken craft. Each grabbed an end. It was waterlogged and heavy but they managed to roll it over. It was the boat that Pocahontas had taken that morning from Werowocomoco but there was no sign of Suckahanna.

"I'm sorry," said Amonsens, seeing how wretched Pocahontas was. "I suppose she must have drowned when it tipped over."

"But then surely her body would be floating here somewhere," said Pocahontas. "Maybe she managed to swim ashore."

"In that storm? You saw how awful it was."

"Just give me a little more time," pleaded Pocahontas. "I can't just leave her."

"All right," agreed Amonsens. "But don't be long. It's almost dusk."

Pocahontas dashed off into the pine forest, shouting "Suckahanna" as loudly as she could. The light was fading and the temperature was dropping fast. Her hair was still sopping wet and freezing water was trickling down her back.

The huge trees grew so densely together that she could not move in a straight line, but she made sure that she could see the edge of the creek. The shoreline curved sharply inwards. *Perhaps she's there*, thought Pocahontas, but it was only another expanse of muddy water. Her spirits sank and she slowed down. She called out "Suckahanna" one last time, but her heart was no longer in it. It was hopeless. She turned around and headed back towards Amonsens. But as she threaded her way between the trees she realized she'd lost sight of the water. Every way she turned looked the same: black tree trunks and a forest floor covered with waist-high bracken. It was disorientating. She could be only a few hundred yards away from the water but now she'd lost sight of it, she might never find it again.

Stop thinking like that! Pocahontas told herself. *Try to work out where you are!*

She must have been heading east when she left Amonsens, so now she needed to head west. The sky should be a little lighter that way. She looked up through the towering trees. Wasn't the patch of sky to her left just a little bit brighter? Soon the pines thinned out slightly and now she could see water to her left. Thank Okeus! She ran the last few feet and emerged, to her surprise, close to the entrance of the creek. She'd overshot Amonsens but now at least she could work her way back along the shore without getting lost again.

Then something caught her eye. It was a trail of glinting wet patches in the muddy earth. Her heart quickened. She hurried over and there, coming out of the mud and onto the sandy earth, were footprints! Footprints heading from the water into the woods! The indentations were half-full of water and the edges were soft and blurred, but they were definitely human.

She waved and shouted excitedly in Amonsens's direction.

"Come quickly!"

Amonsens began paddling over, dragging the second canoe behind her. As soon as her sister waded ashore, Pocahontas followed the trail. At first the prints were well defined but soon they were lost in the thick bracken. Suckahanna could have gone in any direction.

"Suckahanna!" Pocahontas shouted at the top of her voice. "Can you hear me?"

A twig crackled.

Pocahontas swung round as Suckahanna's face appeared through the bracken. "There you are! What happened?"

"A wave caught me. I was trying to get to land but it came from nowhere, and I fell out of the boat and hurt my foot. I only just made it to the shore. And all the roots are gone."

"Don't worry about that," said Pocahontas. "Are you all right?"

Suckahanna shook her head. "My ankle is badly twisted. I can't walk. You'll have to leave me here."

"No. You can't be left alone."

Pocahontas's mind was racing. Suckahanna needed taking to safety, or a cougar or wolf would find her before the night was out. But then she'd need looking after. Who could do it?

Suddenly she thought of her twin – Tassore. She'd be perfect and together they could escape her father's clutches. But there was one big problem: Tassore was a prisoner. Somehow Pocahontas would have to free her – tonight.

31

POCHAHONTAS dashed back to the creek, where Amonsens was lashing the canoe to a tree.

"I've found her," she said simply. "You must go home. If you leave now, you'll be back before dusk."

"Don't you need any more help?"

"No. I've got the other boat now, thanks to you. I'll be fine."

By the time Pocahontas and Suckahanna reached the last bend in the Mattaponi River before Werowocomoco, the sky was black. Only a sliver of a crescent moon, shining dimly through a blanket of clouds, lit the murky bleak water. Pocahontas had lost all sense of time. Was it past midnight? She had no idea.

Silently, she steered the canoe towards the reeds that lined the riverbank. There was a rustle of bending stems as it ran aground.

"Suckahanna, wait here," she whispered and then she crept off along the gloomy trail.

The walls of Werowocomoco loomed ahead. *Getting in is the easy part*, thought Pocahontas as she followed the worn track towards the town's only entrance. The problem was how to get out – with Tassore.

She was less than twenty yards away, when Rawhunt appeared.

"Who's there?" he asked holding up a burning torch and peering into the darkness.

"It's me – Pocahontas."

"Well, hurry up then, miss," said Rawhunt, shooing her through the town walls.

Pocahontas was surprised. She'd been missing all day in a terrible storm. Anything could have happened and Rawhunt didn't even seem to have noticed.

"Is there something wrong?" she asked.

Rawhunt paused.

"I'm sorry to be so rude, miss," he said, "but the whole town is in uproar. This afternoon sixteen of our warriors didn't return home. The palefaces have taken them prisoner."

"Why?"

"John Smith is demanding that every spade, sword and knife be returned to Jamestown before they are released."

"Oh no," said Pocahontas. The Powhatans now relied on the tools they had stolen from the palefaces. "What's Father going to do?"

"This evening we captured a couple of their men in the forest but it's bound to lead to trouble. Now get to bed, miss. At least you're safely home. That's one less thing to worry about."

Pocahontas walked across the silent square towards the daughters' yi-hakan. She glanced over her shoulder. Rawhunt was heading back towards the gate. She waited in the shadows and only once she was certain he'd gone did she turn and creep along the walls of the meeting lodge. All was quiet. No fire could be seen between the gaps in the wicker walls; her father must have retired for the night. Apart from the guards patrolling its walls, Werowocomoco was asleep. Good. That was just what she wanted.

She tiptoed away from the House of Bones and past another cluster of huts. Ahead of her were the slave yi-hakans. *This is it*, she thought, picking out the one closest to the wall. *This is where Tassore will be.*

Cautiously she crouched down and lifted the mat that hung across the doorway. There, just by the entrance and alarmingly close, was Pochins, the slave master. He was a bear of a man, scowling even as he slept and snoring so heavily she could feel his warm stale breath on her cheek. Her heart began to pound; if only he didn't sleep in *this* yi-hakan. She peered beyond him. Embers were glowing dully in the hearth and she could just make out the outlines of rows of sleeping bodies. In the dingy light it was impossible to tell which one was Tassore. She'd have to go further inside.

Be as silent as a deer, she told herself as she crept into the dark room, inching slowly past Pochins and then shuffling forwards on her stomach between two rows of feet. The gap was just wide enough for her to squeeze through but if anyone stretched or rolled over they would feel her.

She wriggled her way down a quarter of the length of the yi-hakan, then pulled herself up onto her elbows and peeked at the faces. There was the old slave she often saw working in the fields and next to him a wrinkled hunched woman. Tassore had to be further in. Pocahontas crawled forward until she reached the circle of stones around the hearth where the cinders glowed a dusty orange. She was going to have to climb over the remains of the fire. Slowly, gingerly, she got onto her knees and it was then that she saw Tassore. She was just beyond the fire, lying flat on her back with her mouth open. The girl on her left was less than an inch from her shoulder but luckily the other neighbour was on his front, facing the other way.

Pocahontas stepped carefully over the warm hearth. How could she possibly wake Tassore without waking that girl? Gently she tried stroking the sole of Tassore's foot. Nothing. She did it again, more firmly. Tassore jerked her foot as if flicking a fly. *This is no good*, thought Pocahontas and, holding her breath, she gave Tassore a firm pinch on the ankle. Tassore yanked her foot in towards her body. *Please wake up*, thought Pocahontas. *Please look this way.*

Sleepily, Tassore lifted her head up. Pocahontas held her fingers to her lips, silently imploring her not to make a sound. Tassore stared ahead, opened her mouth and then, just when Pocahontas was sure she would scream, she nodded. Dizzy with relief, Pocahontas motioned for her to follow. Slowly, slowly, Tassore extricated herself from her neighbours, moving as delicately as a cougar, until at last she was crouching behind Pocahontas.

"Let's go," whispered Pocahontas. "I'll explain when we're outside."

They were halfway towards the entrance when there was a blood-curdling scream.

"The palefaces are coming! We're under attack!" It was Rawhunt. "Everyone up!"

For a moment Pocahontas thought they might get out before Pochins awoke, but his great bulk was already blocking the doorway. They were trapped.

32

"WHAT are *you* doing here?" demanded Pochins, spraying Pocahontas with beads of spit. "And Tassore, where do you think you're going?"

Pocahontas was speechless. She dreaded to think what her father would do to them both when he found out.

Just then there were more shouts from outside.

"The palefaces are coming! They're burning the boats!"

"You two, wait here!" Pochins ordered, snatching up a tomahawk. "Kalim, watch them. The rest of you, get up!"

Once Pochins and the slaves had left, Pocahontas and Tassore huddled together under the disdainful eye of their guard. Kalim was a morose man but he was tough and reliable, and always did exactly what his master said.

There was another loud crash, alarmingly close to the yi-hakan. Kalim hurried outside to investigate.

As soon as they were alone, Pocahontas whispered, "Tassore, your sister is alive. I haven't been able to tell you because Pochins never leaves you alone but tonight I had to take the chance. Suckahanna's been hurt. She needs your help."

Before Tassore could respond there was another loud

thump and then, without warning, the yi-hakan was on fire. Hungry flames licked the straw walls and in moments the hut was filled with choking smoke.

"Quick!" said Pocahontas, grabbing Tassore's hand and pulling her out just as the saplings supporting the yi-hakan collapsed.

They emerged, spluttering and coughing, their faces covered in soot. Kalim had disappeared and everywhere men and women were running this way and that, trying desperately to put out the fires that dotted the town. Pocahontas grabbed the arm of a harassed-looking woman, one of her father's cooks.

"What's happened?" she asked.

"The palefaces have ambushed us, miss. They shot burning torches over the walls and then ran off. Your father's just given orders for all women and children to leave before the place turns into a furnace." And with that she scuttled away.

Realizing that no one would notice them in the chaos, Pocahontas seized Tassore's hand and pulled her into the crowd streaming towards the gate. She was relieved that Tassore was keeping up with the rush; all that was left of her injury was an ugly scar and a slight limp.

"Keep your head down," Pocahontas whispered as they were squeezed into the narrow entrance. She counted her way past the guards. One, two, three, almost there ... four. They'd done it! But as they stumbled out of the crush and into the pasture, Pocahontas saw a face she recognized. Wassacan's thin neck was turning this way and that, no doubt searching for the chief's daughters. It wouldn't be long before she spotted them, so Pocahontas quickly pulled Tassore away from the fleeing crowds and towards the river.

At last they reached the muddy trail. Pocahontas was relieved but she felt little joy. Orange sparks drifted into the night sky and charred lumps of wood were all that remained of the Powhatans' fine canoes. Her tribe was in danger and the palefaces, the very men she'd fed and sustained for the past two moons, were responsible. Okeus's terrible prophesy was coming true.

33

TASSORE was the first to spot the outline of the small canoe, sticking out from a clump of reeds. She flung herself into the boat and hugged her twin sister as if she'd never let go.

Pocahontas sat down at the water's edge, not wanting to intrude, until at last Tassore called out, "Come here."

She clambered into the wobbling boat.

"Come with us," said Tassore, her eyes shining brightly. "We'll hide in the House of Bones at the waterfall and cross the Quirank Mountains when Suckahanna's strong enough."

Pocahontas was tempted. She wouldn't have her father controlling her every move. She wouldn't end up married to someone as awful as Arakum. But in her heart she knew she couldn't leave. The Powhatans were her people.

"Thank you, but I can't," she said.

"Why not?"

"I can't desert my tribe at a moment like this."

"But if you go back, your father will punish you."

"I don't care," said Pocahontas. Her mind was made up. She'd had enough of deception and dishonesty. "I'm going to go straight to Father to tell him everything. Only then will I be able to help."

"Help with what?" asked Tassore.

"Help stop Okeus's prophesy from coming true."

"But what can you do?" asked Suckahanna. "You're only thirteen winters' old."

"I know," said Pocahontas, "but John Smith owes me his life twice over. Namontack told me that he was a practical man and all he cares about is that Jamestown survives. Somehow I've got to use that."

"Then we must come with you," said Tassore, getting to her feet.

Pocahontas was horrified. This was the last thing she wanted. After all this time, the twins were finally together and free. However much she would miss them, she mustn't jeopardize that.

"No," she said, with absolute determination. "My father made a terrible mistake when he ordered the massacre of your tribe. Your escape is the only way for me to make amends."

"But we can't leave you," protested Tassore.

"You can and you must. Go now! It's the perfect time."

And she jumped out of the canoe and pushed it away from the riverbank before Tassore or Suckahanna could stop her. In no time the boat caught the current and began drifting off.

"Pocahontas, I'll never forget you," called Tassore with tears in her eyes. "You're the best friend I've ever had."

"And I'll never forget you," said Pocahontas.

She stood watching the canoe float away until it was impossible to distinguish it from the inky black river. Tassore and Suckahanna were free and now it was time to face her father.

DAWN was breaking as Pocahontas returned to Werowocomoco. It was a wretched sight. Overnight, the fields surrounding the town had been transformed into a bleak, makeshift camp. Everywhere, children were sitting listlessly on furs while their weary mothers, aunts and grandparents looked dazed.

Pocahontas picked her way through the refugees. As she got closer to the town the air became increasingly acrid. A hideous stench of burnt hair and fat caught the back of her throat. She passed through the walls and found Werowocomoco had been devastated. The guards' lodgings, the store rooms, the slaves' yi-hakans and the sweat hut were scorched patches of earth. Here and there bewildered families were searching through the charred remains of their homes. Only the meeting lodge seemed untouched. That must be where her father was.

Pocahontas took a deep breath and approached it, hoping the guards wouldn't dare challenge a daughter of the chief. She was relieved when they nodded her in, but now came the hard part – getting her father to listen to what she had to say.

At the far end of the chamber, Chanco and Chief

Powhatan were sitting on either side of the fire while Otta was kneeling, fanning her father.

"Brother, we *must* attack the palefaces tonight," Chanco was saying, thumping his fist for emphasis.

Just then Otta spotted Pocahontas. Despite last night's chaos, she still managed to look neat and tidy. Her hair was stuck with feathers and the shells on her dress gleamed in the firelight. She stopped flapping the feather fan and said, "Father, there's someone to see you."

Both men turned around.

"How dare you come in here?" asked Chief Powhatan coldly.

"I want to help stop the fighting," Pocahontas answered, keeping her voice as steady as she could. "The palefaces owe me their lives. For two moons, I've taken corn to them. I think they will listen to me."

"Why did you do that?" asked Chanco.

"They were starving and I didn't want Namontack to go hungry."

"Then you've been stealing from us?" said her father.

"No, sir," said Pocahontas hurriedly. "I used abandoned Chesepiock corn. Father, please give me a chance."

"Your tales are too preposterous." Her father was almost shouting. "Fed all the palefaces... Saved their lives... I've never heard anything so ridiculous. Either you've been with Wassacan or collecting tuckahoes. Guards!" Immediately four warriors entered the longhouse. "Take Pocahontas away!" ordered Chief Powhatan.

"I'll deal with her later."

Oh no, thought Pocahontas. And then from nowhere Amonsens appeared.

"Father, she's telling the truth," said her tiny sister in the same determined way she'd spoken to Otta at the creek.

"How would you know?" demanded the chief dismissively.

"Because I saw it with my own eyes. She hasn't been collecting tuckahoes. She's had someone else do it." She turned to Pocahontas. "Forgive me, but last night I didn't leave when you told me to. I had to know you were all right so I waited and then followed you. It was too dark to see who you were with, but I think you're going to have to tell Father."

The chief rolled his eyes. "Well?" he asked irritably.

Pocahontas took a deep breath and told him everything... Her worries about the prophecy, her shame at the Chesepiock raid, why she'd helped free Tassore and how she'd ended up helping the palefaces in order to save Namontack.

Her father listened in silence, sucking thoughtfully on his pipe and occasionally blowing blue smoke rings.

"So, if we are to believe you," he said at last, "you know the palefaces better than any of us. Would they return our warriors, if you asked, after all that you've done for them?"

"I don't know," said Pocahontas truthfully. "But Father,

there's nothing lost by letting me try."

"You can't allow this," said Chanco, standing up and pacing around the fire. "It would be demeaning to send a child to beg for us, and what of the prophecy? If these palefaces are the nation Okeus warned of, we should attack them."

"Brother, their weapons are too strong," said Chief Powhatan, suddenly looking his seventy winters. "Look at the damage they have already done to Werowocomoco. Okeus is a tricky god... He said a nation would arise from Chesepiock Bay and destroy us... But perhaps we are provoking them. If we leave the palefaces alone, maybe they will become good neighbours."

"That will never happen."

"Chanco, one night you will inherit the empire, but until then I am its chief and it is for me to decide. It must be better for our people to sleep easy than to lie awake each night wondering whether the snap of a twig means the palefaces are coming to get us. For that reason I will give Pocahontas a chance." He turned to his daughter. "You will go to them early tomorrow with Rawhunt. Good luck."

POCAHONTAS and Rawhunt paused at the edge of the forest. Ahead of them was the clearing and beyond it the walls of Jamestown.

"That's it," said Pocahontas. "We should change here, where they can't see us."

That morning they'd jogged across the peninsula in leggings and were now splattered with mud. Pocahontas had no idea how she would be received by John Smith and the palefaces, but it would surely help if she looked like a chief's daughter. From a knapsack she pulled out some clean moccasins and her finest dress, the one her grandmother had given her all those moons ago. She slipped into the soft suede and wove two beautiful green and red parakeet feathers into her single plait.

"How do I look?" she asked anxiously.

"Like a true daughter of Chief Powhatan. What about me?"

Pocahontas had never seen Rawhunt look so grand. He'd wiped the worst of the mud from his shins and painted his face with blue and silver stripes. Around his shoulders he wore a luxurious fur coat and his loincloth was hung with shark teeth.

"You look fine," she said.

She stepped into the clearing, with Rawhunt one step behind. She was less than halfway across the meadow when the wooden gate creaked open. John Smith was standing in the doorway with his hands in his pockets.

"I wasn't expecting you," he said. "It's not the fifth night."

"I'm not bringing corn," said Pocahontas. "I bring a message from Chief Powhatan."

Smith's eyes narrowed.

"Your father? What does he want?"

"He wishes you to free our warriors."

"He's sent a child to plead for him," said Smith, shaking his head in disbelief. "Tell your father, if he wants his warriors back, he must come and beg for them himself."

Pocahontas took a moment to compose herself. Didn't this man realize who her father was? Chief Powhatan would never demean himself by coming to Jamestown. John Smith didn't seem to understand that he was werowance of the mightiest empire in the world – but surely he would realize that war between the palefaces and the Powhatans would be disastrous for his precious Jamestown, so she said, "Sir, if you do not release our warriors, my father will be honour-bound to attack you and there will be war between our two tribes."

"If there's war, we shall win," said Smith.

"In war, nobody wins," said Pocahontas, thinking of Namontack's father and poor Tassore and Suckahanna.

"But if you let our warriors return with me, my father promises peace."

Smith eyed her steadily. She could almost feel him calculating whether to agree or not and so she quickly added, "And if there is peace, Chief Powhatan will allow you to trade for food, because you should know, my father will not permit me to bring corn any more."

"How do I know I can trust the chief?" asked John Smith.

"He has sent me here with no protection other than a single scout. He has shown more trust than you."

"And if I don't agree?"

"Our village is destroyed, but perhaps yours will be as well. Sir, I have saved your life twice over. Don't you owe me this?"

Smith stroked his beard thoughtfully.

"I will spare your warriors," he said at last. "But now you and I are even. Once Namontack returns, I owe you nothing."

It was evening by the time Pocahontas, Rawhunt and the sixteen warriors entered Werowocomoco. The square was crowded with Powhatans, joyfully cheering the return of their men. As Pocahontas made her way through the crowd, she was warmly congratulated and slapped on the back.

"Come to the lodge," someone shouted. "Your father is waiting for you."

Chief Powhatan was seated on a deerskin rug with Otta at his feet. Pocahontas walked slowly forwards and then dropped to her knees in front of the dais.

"Pocahontas, you have succeeded where many grown men might have failed," said her father in his gravelly voice. "You are a worthy daughter of mine and you shall be my favourite once more. Otta, move!"

Pocahontas's heart sank. This was the last thing she was expecting and the last thing she wanted. She longed to be free ... and so she swallowed hard and said, "Father, being your favourite daughter is a great honour, but when you first heard my name you said then its meaning was both good and bad. Do you not think that perhaps I am too mischievous for you?"

Chief Powhatan looked surprised. "You mean you don't want to be favourite?"

She shook her head.

"No, sir."

Her father looked troubled. "But surely there is some way I can thank you."

"There is. Namontack never intended to harm you or the tribe. When he returns, please forgive him."

"I will, but what about you? Isn't there anything you want for yourself?"

Pocahontas knew exactly what she yearned for – to go home to her grandmother and her crammed yi-hakan far from the grandeur of Werowocomoco and the troublesome palefaces.

"There is one thing," she said tentatively. "Would you let me return to Hatto, sir? My grandmother is old and I want to take care of her."

"Is that all?"

"Yes," said Pocahontas. "Nothing would make me happier."

Chief Powhatan leaned forward and patted her affectionately on the head.

"I will miss you, but I grant you your wish. Pocahontas, you will return home with my blessing but here in Werowocomoco and throughout the empire I will make sure we remember your brave deeds forever. Thanks to you, we will live in peace with our neighbours and Okeus's prophecy will not come true."

POCAHONTAS was standing on the banks of the wide Pamunkey River. It was early morning and an icy wind was blowing across the plain. She dipped a toe in the water and withdrew it sharply. It was freezing.

"I'll hold your cloak while you swim," said Keffgore, sitting on a rock near the shore.

The old woman stretched out a wrinkled arm.

"Hold on," said Pocahontas, gazing towards the bend in the river. "Someone's coming."

A figure in a canoe was paddling towards them. It was a man. He waved and suddenly Pocahontas realized who it was. Namontack! He was back at last!

One moon after she'd returned to Hatto, her father sent Rawhunt to tell her that Namontack had returned safely from across the Great Sea and would shortly be attempting the Huskanaw.

The canoe ran aground and Namontack waded ashore. Immediately Pocahontas noticed that his cheeks had hollowed out, his torso was leaner and he had the broad shoulders of a hunter.

"I can't believe you're home!" she said excitedly. "Grandmother, look at him! He must be a warrior now."

"Is that true?" asked Keffgore with a gummy smile. "Did you pass the Huskanaw?"

Namontack nodded shyly.

"And will you now stay in Hatto?"

"Yes. I've come to join my mother and sisters. Now that I can hunt deer, they won't have to rely on charity." He turned to Pocahontas. "Will you come with me to tell them?"

"I'd be honoured," she answered, taking his outstretched hand.

As they walked along the winding trail through the grassy meadows, Pocahontas thought of all that had happened in the past two winters. The terrible raid on the Chesepiocks, the arrival of the strange palefaces and their attacks on the Powhatans. But at least Okeus's dreadful prophecy had not come true, and she and Namontack were safely home in Hatto where they belonged.

They reached the outskirts of the village. Ahead of them smoke was rising from Namontack's yi-hakan. His mother would be inside stirring a pot of corn bread and Pocahontas couldn't wait to see the look on her face when her son returned.

THE END

WHAT HAPPENED NEXT

AFTER Namontack's return to North America in September 1608, Pocahontas had little further contact with either John Smith or the colonists and so for some years she disappears into historical obscurity.

We know more about John Smith. He continued to try to persuade the lazy colonists to work, but despite his efforts, by spring 1609 Jamestown's inhabitants were in trouble. They only just made it through the lean winter months by eating the last of their meagre stores and raiding Native American supplies.

In August 1609, ships arrived from London bringing a further six hundred colonists to Jamestown. Their arrival confirmed Chanco (more formally known as Opechancanuff) in his view that the English were a danger and must be got rid of before it was too late. Chief Powhatan was finally convinced of this and ordered that the English be starved from his lands. To show how serious he was, an entire tribe was slaughtered for selling grain to the colonists.

Despite Chief Powhatan's decree, by harvesting their own crops, using new supplies from London, and forcing the aristocrats in the camp to work with the words, "He that shall not work, shall not eat," John Smith managed to keep the Jamestown colony going. During this period, he also explored the huge Chesepiock Bay, in a fruitless search for a river leading to the Pacific Ocean. He kept detailed diaries on these journeys, describing the Native American landscape, towns, their cultures and traditions. Smith also drew many maps, recording the Powhatan names for mountains, rivers and villages. Many of these names are still in use today, including the Potomac, the river that runs through Washington, DC, and Chesepiock Bay, now anglicized to Chesapeake Bay.

In September 1609, John Smith was returning from an expedition when a spark from a musket drifted onto a gunpowder bag hanging from his belt. The bag exploded and John Smith was horribly burned. He was taken back to Jamestown, where he made a partial recovery, but his wounds were still painfully infected and he returned to England on the next passing ship. A rumour spread among the Native Americans that the much-feared John Smith had died. Pocahontas must have been told but we have no record of how she felt about his reported death.

After Smith's departure, rivalry and ill-discipline spread through Jamestown, leaving the colonists dreadfully vulnerable as their supplies dwindled once more. The winter of 1609–10 was a terrible one and became known as the Starving Time. Disease and hunger devastated the settlers. Colonists were reduced to eating cats and dogs, and then rats and mice, and finally shoe leather and even the starch in their stiff white collars. In their desperation, some also turned to cannibalism. Fresh corpses were dug up and eaten. One man, Henry Collins, is said to have murdered his pregnant wife and feasted on her.

When four more ships arrived from England the following May, only sixty of the six hundred settlers were still alive and all wanted to return home. However, when they saw the new supplies of food, medicine and healthy people, they were persuaded to stay. Order was restored under a strong leader called Baron De La Warr, and by the following summer the colony of Jamestown finally began to thrive.

Although there are no historical records of Pocahontas during the period from 1609 to 1613, this was not the end of her extraordinary tale or her dealings with the colonists. Despite saving the inhabitants of Jamestown from starvation in the winter of 1608, the English found a strange way to repay her. In April 1613, Pocahontas, now eighteen years old, was visiting a relative in the outlying village of Passapatanzy when a trader called Samuel Argall sailed into town. Hearing of her presence, Argall decided his luck was in. With a copper kettle and glass beads, he bribed the chief of the village to bring Pocahontas to his boat. Here she was kidnapped and carted off to Jamestown.

News of Pocahontas's capture spread like wildfire. Chief Powhatan offered bushels of corn, weapons and stolen tools in exchange for her return but the English refused, saying it was not enough.

Months passed with no agreement while Pocahontas

was kept prisoner in the remote colonist town of Henricus. Finally, March 1614, almost a year after the kidnapping, the English finally agreed to Chief Powhatan's terms. They brought Pocahontas to the Pamunkey River, where her father was waiting, but she had a surprise in store for him and her captors. When brought ashore, she refused to speak except to declare that if her father truly loved her he would have got her back sooner. Since he had not, she would not be returning. She would remain with the colonists.

Historians debated the reasons for Pocahontas's extraordinary decision. She might truly have been so offended by her father's reluctance to offer more for her that she decided to make the best of it with the settlers. Other theories include her attraction to Christianity and the colonist way of life, but the most likely explanation is that after spending more than a year isolated from her own people, she had fallen in love. The man was John Rolfe, a gentle, devout, twenty-eight-year-old farmer.

Whatever the reason, Pocahontas returned to Henricus and shortly afterwards was baptized, becoming the first native in English America to convert to Christianity. At her baptism ceremony she was given the new name of "Rebecca".

A month later, she married John Rolfe. After the marriage, the first of its kind in North America between a native and a settler, relations between the English and the Powhatan tribes entered a golden age. Settlers and native people lived happily side-by-side, farming, hunting, trading and perhaps socializing together, and Chief Powhatan promised never to wage war on the English again.

In the spring of 1616, Pocahontas and John Rolfe made the long ocean crossing to England, accompanied by their young son, Thomas. The trip was paid for by a tobacco company keen to use an exotic Native American princess to generate interest in England in growing tobacco in the new colony, just as they had used Namontack eight years earlier.

After spending some time in the busy port of Plymouth, Pocahontas and her husband journeyed to London. It is hard to imagine what she thought of England as she travelled across the country by carriage. For the first time she saw cattle, horses, carts, roads, wheels and finally a city.

London at this time had a population of more than two hundred thousand people. It was a bustling place with narrow streets and tall buildings, some of them over six stories high, as well as theatres, fancy shops and cathedrals. It also had appalling poverty and terrible sanitation. Pocahontas would have been used to wood smoke, but coal smog and open sewers would have been new and unpleasant.

News of her arrival preceded her and Londoners were curious to see a "real Red Indian". Pocahontas was treated like a princess. She was received at court by King James and Queen Anne and attended many plays and balls. She also learned that John Smith had not been killed but was in fact alive and living in England and a reunion was arranged.

In March 1617, after almost a year in England, Pocahontas began the long journey back to North America with her husband and young son, now two years old. They sailed along the River Thames but by the time their ship reached Kent, Pocahontas was seriously ill. The London air had never agreed with her and she'd probably contracted pneumonia or tuberculosis. The family were forced to abandon ship.

Pocahontas died in an unknown inn on 21 March, 1617 and was buried that same day in the medieval graveyard of St George's church, Gravesend. She was just twenty-two years old.

John Smith continued to write about the New World and made two further trips to North America to a region he named New England. He died in 1631 at the age of fifty-one.

John Rolfe returned to America, leaving his two-year-old son in Kent. Thomas survived into adulthood, but never saw his father again. Meanwhile, Rolfe became a pioneer in the tobacco trade. He was one of the first colonists to send tobacco back to England. By 1618 the crop was profitable and popular, and colonists were flocking to the New World to start their own farms.

Pocahontas's father, Chief Powhatan, died around a year after his daughter. He was succeeded by his brother,

Chanco. The new chief believed that, although relations with settlers were friendly, the colonists remained a danger to his tribes. Each year more English arrived, grabbing precious land to grow tobacco. He decided to deal with them and so one fateful day in March 1622, he ordered his men to attack the settlers. It is estimated that more than four hundred colonists were brutally slaughtered by axes, tomahawks, hammers and saws.

If Chanco thought this would send the remainder running, it was a terrible miscalculation. The English were provoked and responded. Soldiers were sent from England to exterminate the Powhatans. Colonists raided native villages, burning homes, crops and canoes, and Chanco was captured and killed.

By 1646, only forty years after John Smith and his fellow colonists first landed in North America, the Powhatans were fugitives in their own land. By 1700 they had all but disappeared – murdered, driven away or killed by diseases such as measles, smallpox and chickenpox, to which they had no immunity and which were brought by later English colonists. And so, despite Pocahontas's efforts to bridge the two cultures, Japazaw's terrible prophesy was fulfilled – the Powhatan empire was destroyed by a people arising from the tip of the Chesepiock Bay.

AUTHOR'S NOTES

WHEN I first began to research the early years of Pocahontas's life, I found that there was little to rely on before the fateful landings of the *Susan Constant*, *Godspeed* and *Discovery*, the ships bringing the first English colonists to Virginia. However, from that time detailed records and diaries were kept by a number of the colonists and from these and Native American oral traditions, historians have been able to find out a lot about the culture and traditions of the Powhatan people.

When writing this story I have tried to be historically accurate about the lives of the Powhatans and the English colonists, as well as the key characters of the period. Pocahontas, Chief Powhatan, Japazaw, Chanco, Namontack, Parahunt, Rawhunt, Edward-Maria Wingfield, Tom Savage and John Smith are all real people but, of course, in most instances I've had to imagine their personalities. We do have some clues from the past. Chief Powhatan is described in Smith's diary as having "such a majesty as I cannot express, nor yet have often seen, either in pagan or Christian". John Smith was determined to keep Jamestown going, despite many of his men wanting to abandon the colony. Japazaw did forecast the arrival of a terrible enemy in Chesepiock Bay resulting in the slaughter of the Chesepiock tribe. Chanco was steadfastly hostile to the colonists and led a savage uprising against them soon after inheriting the throne. Namontack was sent to live in Jamestown and then sailed to England. Finally, Pocahontas must have been spirited, intelligent and brave. When only a child, she dramatically saved John Smith's life, stopped the colonists from starving during their first winter in North America and secured the release of sixteen Powhatan warriors, preventing further bloodshed and later, after her marriage to a settler, she forged links between two clashing cultures that endured until her untimely death.

NOTES FROM THE PAST

HOMES: The Powhatans called their homes yi-hakans. They were built in mulberry groves, which shaded them from the burning sun during the long, hot summer and gave them some shelter from the terrible storms that lashed the area in winter. The houses were made from woven reed thatching over bent sapling branches. They had rounded sides, making them wind, rain and snow resistant. Extended families lived together in a single room where they worked, cooked and stored goods. Bedding was made from animal skins and mats. A central fire was used for cooking and warmth but the huts would have been very smoky and the living conditions cramped, with little privacy.

CHILDHOOD: As soon as Powhatan children could walk they began to learn the skills necessary to survive in the woods. From the age of six, boys would hunt and track, and were not given breakfast until they succeeded at their bow and arrow target practice. Girls helped the women gather food, cook, make clothes and build homes. Most girls were married by the age of thirteen.

NAMES: The Powhatans did not have surnames. A baby was initially given a name by its father. As the child grew older it would earn a second name from its character or exploits. Pocahontas's formal name is believed to have been "Amonute" (meaning unknown today) but she is remembered by her second name – Pocahontas – meaning "mischievous", "little wanton" or "laughing and joyous one", due to her feisty, fun and inquisitive nature.

THE HUSKANAW: For a Powhatan boy to become a man he had to undertake the Huskanaw, usually when aged around fifteen. This was a gruelling initiation rite that started with a day-long festival in the woods after which the boys were led away by priests. They would not be seen for many months. During this time they were intoxicated with roots, kept in cages and had their memories ritually erased. They were also trained in religion and hunting skills. If they passed various arduous tests they were "reborn" as warriors. Only then could they return to their families, marry, join the deer hunt and become advisers to the chiefs.

The Huskanaw was extremely tough. Each year some boys did not survive its rigours. These unfortunates were sacrificed to Okeus.

FOOD: Before the arrival of Europeans, there were no domesticated animals in North America. This meant there were no horses, cows, goats, sheep, chickens or pigs and so all meat had to be hunted. Using spears, wooden traps and nets, the Powhatan men fished and hunted for sea bass, salmon, turtles, clams, crabs, deer, rabbits, raccoons and wild turkeys. Women gathered berries, roots, wild fruits and nuts. The Powhatans supplemented their diet during the summer by growing corn, beans and squashes, and in spring they relied on pulling tuckahoe roots from the many creeks lining the bay.

LANGUAGE: The Powhatans lived in the modern day American states of Virginia and Maryland. They spoke dialects that belonged to the Algonquian language – a language that extended from Canada right down the eastern coast of the United States and as far west as the Great Plains.

Unusually among the English that arrived in Chesapeake Bay, John Smith was an accomplished linguist. During the ten years before his American adventure he'd learnt Dutch, Hungarian and Turkish while fighting as a soldier in a number of European wars. This probably helped him quickly learn the Algonquian language.

POWHATAN CALENDAR: The Powhatans divided the year into five seasons – *wassacan* or winter, which began with the return of the migratory geese, *cattapeuk* or spring, *cohattayough* or summer, the main season for planting, *nepinough* or harvest and *taquitock* or leaf-fall, a time of feasts and sacrifice.

Time was tracked by making notches on sticks as well as following the movement of the moon and the stars.

A full year was called a "winter", a full month, a "moon" and a full day, a "night". A day was divided into sunrise, noon, sunset and midnight.

CHIEFS: A Powhatan chief inherited his position through his mother's line. It was for this reason that Chanco was heir to his brother, Chief Powhatan. The next in line after this generation of brothers was not their children, but the son of one of their sisters. This was for two practical reasons. Firstly, chiefs had many wives and therefore could have children born almost simultaneously. Secondly, the Powhatan system meant that there was rarely a child monarch, as the chief's nephews had plenty of time to reach adulthood. Thus, although the Europeans thought of Pocahontas as a princess, she could never have inherited the Powhatan throne.

RELIGION: The Powhatans worshipped a number of spirits, the main ones being Ahone, Okeus and the Sun. Okeus was a worrisome, punishing spirit. Ahone was calm and kindly, and the Sun was the giver of life. The Powhatans would stand in a circle around a pile of dried tobacco at sunrise and sunset and pray. These prayers would be led by the tribe's priest and senior adviser to its chief. A dried blackbird tied into his hair above his ear was his badge of office. He would also have a distinctive haircut – shaved except for two short tufts above his forehead, which were stiffened with bear's grease, with a mohawk running from his forehead to the nape of his neck.

PLACES OF WORSHIP: These were built on an east-west axis and were known as the House of Bones. They were divided into two rooms. The first room had a hearth in its centre with a permanent fire – a gift from the sun. It was used as a meeting place for the leader of the tribe and the living quarters of the priest. The second, more sacred, room was dismal and dark. Here the Powhatans stored wooden statues of their gods and the bodies of past chiefs. These were preserved by peeling away the skin and disembowelling the organs. The flesh was then scraped away from the bones using shells. The skeleton and skin were dried in the sun and then the skeleton was put back into the skin and filled out with sand. The resulting mummy was hung with copper and pearl chains and bracelets and placed on a platform at the western end of the House of Bones.

SACRIFICES: The Powhatans made sacrifices to ward off evil and as thanksgiving for the harvest or good fortune. These sacrifices included precious objects such as shells, beads, tobacco, deer suet and copper but also animals and, in extreme cases, humans. Human sacrificial practices included dashing out brains with rocks, burning alive and dismemberment.

HEALTH: The Powhatans had no horses and so the only means of transport were by canoe and on foot. Consequently they prized fast runners and were wiry, fit and strong. The Powhatans were also hygienic, taking daily baths in the river, believing this built their strength.

The first Europeans would have been physically unimpressive to the Powhatans. Their diet was inferior and so they were shorter and their health was generally poorer. In addition, they rarely bathed or washed their heavy woollen and linen clothes and so were covered with lice and fleas.

MEDICINE: Like the Europeans that sailed into Chesapeake Bay, the Powhatans had little understanding of modern medicine. Instead they believed in the power of sacrifice and magic to cure injuries and disease and they also had a detailed knowledge of the plants growing in the forests and used many of them as cures, including liverwort for wounds, trout lily for swellings and foxglove for snakebites.

EUROPEAN ILLNESSES: Diseases such as measles, chickenpox and smallpox developed in the towns of Europe, where people and domesticated animals lived crowded together in unsanitary conditions. Over hundreds of years, Europeans developed resistance to these infections, making them unpleasant but not lethal. Unfortunately for the Native Americans they had no such immunity. In later years, when the colonists arrived in North America in large numbers, they inevitably brought their germs with them and gradually these spread with devastating effect. Historians estimate that more than eighty per cent of all Native Americans were killed by European infections.

Before they were famous ... meet Cleopatra, who will one day be the Queen of Egypt, in this new series about the early lives of some of history's most charismatic figures.

A young girl flees the city, fearing for her life. Living in hiding, uncertain of her future, she finally receives news from home. The time has come to face her enemies – and take her place as Princess Cleopatra, future Queen of Egypt.

"The focus is on providing factual information within an historical context that gives a flavour of the times while delivering a first-rate story." Publishing News

Before they were famous ... meet Boudica, one day to be England's warrior queen, in this new series about the early lives of some of history's most charismatic figures.

In Ancient Britain, a tribesman's daughter is in trouble. The Romans have invaded, her father has been accused of murder and she doesn't know who to trust. When a mysterious druid appears in her village, she knows she must enter his murky world if she is to bring honour to her tribe and one day become Boudica, warrior queen.

BY CAROLINE CORBY

Before they were famous ... meet Willam, one day to be William the Conqueror, Duke of Normandy, in this series about the early lives of some of history's most charismatic figures.

A young boy is sent away to France, far from the political turmoil of the Normandy court. He spends his years training to become a knight and learning the value of friendship and loyalty – which will be vital when he decides he must return to take his rightful place as Duke of Normandy.

BY CAROLINE CORBY